ALSO BY CRAIG HOLDEN

The Narcissist's Daughter

The Jazz Bird

Four Corners of Night

The Last Sanctuary

The River Sorrow

MATALA

Craig Holden

SIMON & SCHUSTER
New York London Toronto Sydney

SIMON & SCHUSTER
1230 Avenue of the Americas
New York, NY 10020

This book is a work of fiction. Names, characters, places, and incidents either are products of the author's imagination or are used fictitiously. Any resemblance to actual events or locales or persons, living or dead, is entirely coincidental.

First Simon & Schuster hardcover edition December 2007

For information about special discounts for bulk purchases, please contact Simon & Schuster Special Sales at 1-800-456-6798 or business@simonandschuster.com

Designed by Jaime Putorti

Manufactured in the United States of America

10 9 8 7 6 5 4 3 2 1

Library of Congress Cataloging-in-Publication Data

Holden, Craig.
Matala / Craig Holden.—1st Simon & Schuster hardcover ed.
p. cm.
1. Smuggling—Fiction. I. Title.
PS3558.O347747M38 2008
813'.54—dc22 2007007885
ISBN-13: 978-0-7432-7499-9
ISBN-10: 0-7432-7499-7

For Jim Larson, who once said to me, "Of course you love the idea of having written. We all do. Now maybe you'd better figure out whether or not you love to write."

and

in memory of my compadre,
Chris Smith

We have all of us taken different paths now; but in this, the first great fragmentation of my maturity I feel the confines of my art and my living deepened immeasurably by the memory of them. In thought I achieve them anew; as if only here—this wooden table over the sea under an olive tree, only here can I enrich them as they deserve.

—LAWRENCE DURRELL, *JUSTINE*

Rome

One

ON A CHILLY SUNNY DECEMBER afternoon, Darcy Arlen slipped down Via della Conciliazione, away from the Hotel Abitazione, and slid her hands into her coat pockets. Across the river, she turned south and settled into a quick, steady walk. The headiness of her solitude—stolen while her roommate, Rhonda, was in the shower and the tour guide, Mrs. Abignale, napped—carried her onward into the city. The group was leaving soon for another of the great ruins, the Baths of Caracalla, but Darcy was already tired of ruins and museums and history, and this was only the second city of the seven they were to visit on this month-and-a-half-long tour, a combined birthday and finally-you-graduated-from-high-school-and-only-six-months-late gift from her parents. She knew now she should have expected this.

At first she stayed close to the river so as not to come too near the monuments and ruins in the center of the old city. The embankments of the Tiber curved west and then east again, bringing her close to the Circus Maximus, but once past that, she cut into the city, onto streets she'd never seen. She loved just being in this place, breathing this ancient air.

For a long time she followed the wide Via Ostiense, past the monolithic Cathedral of Saint Paul, until she finally came into a part of the city that was not for tourists: the real city, office towers and high terraced apartment buildings, where real people, Italians, worked and shopped and didn't have to pretend to like speaking English.

She rested on a bench in a small corner park where two young children squatted on the hard-packed dirt, pitching seeds to the pigeons clustered about them. An older woman, their grandmother she guessed, sat nearby. It felt good to sit and breathe. It felt good to be here alone. The titillation of her rebellion, her sneaking off, the tingling it brought to the soles of her feet and her fingers had of course worn away by now, but not the self-satisfaction. She knew it was really out of any proportion to the mildness of the act. It wasn't as if she'd stood up to anyone and said something, as if she'd told Mrs. Abignale, the tour director, to get stuffed because she was almost worse than Darcy's mother, and that was really saying something. It wasn't as if she'd said anything to anyone. Still, sitting there with all these Italians who weren't even looking at her, as if she were just another part of this world, a regular person, she felt, well, contented. And tired. And a little chilly now.

She bought some sticky dates from a street vendor and wandered north again. Later, near the Ostia Station, she gave most of them to a filthy woman begging with her filthier child. She came upon the Vialle Marco Polo and, thinking it ran vaguely in the direction of the hotel, followed it. Now the afternoon was growing thin, the light coming from lower in the sky, and the streets had fallen into shadow.

Her legs ached and her lips stuck to her teeth. She felt a sheen, a membrane of perspiration, coating all of her body. It was a long way back. She imagined having a quiet dinner somewhere, away from the group, maybe with Rhonda if she wasn't sulking too hard at Darcy's having left without her, and then settling into the deep bed and reading herself to sleep. In the morning, early, they would leave for Florence. She passed through a square with a pyramid in it, and the Vialle Marco Polo became the Via Marmorata. She pulled her coat around her and shivered, but ahead now she could see the river. It cheered her. She'd cross it, she decided, see how she felt, and maybe then find a taxi.

On the bridge, which was nearly empty of pedestrians, a young man leaned over the stone parapet, looking into the water. He wore stained work boots, ripped jeans, and a Carhartt work jacket. As she passed him, he glanced at her. Her momentum carried her past even as she drew a sharp breath when the shock of incongruous recognition made her dizzy. From where did she know him? Which life? Which world?

She'd noticed before, when she had traveled to new or foreign places with her parents, that sometimes a face made her look again, startled her with its familiarity. It was never anyone she knew, of course, and she often couldn't even name who she once knew that the face resembled. It was just the mind playing tricks with the broad familiarity that one pocket of humanity bore to another. Perhaps that was this, she thought. It must be. But she stopped in the middle of the bridge over the Tiber on that clear late December afternoon and told herself that this time she was almost certain.

She walked back and stood beside him so that the sleeve of her coat brushed his. He continued to stare down, as if he were watching something particular. She peered over.

"It's just that it's mesmerizing," he said in perfect American.

"Every bit of it," she answered.

He turned to look at her. He had very dark eyes and nearly blond hair that fell across his forehead.

"I'm sorry," she said. "But you look familiar."

He nodded. "I get that."

"No. I know you. I'm sure of it."

He looked back at the water. He said, "You don't know me."

"I think we went to the same high school."

"Did we?"

"Ulysses County, Ohio. Indian Bend?"

He turned around and leaned back against the parapet now, his elbows cocked behind him, and looked across the bridge and down the river toward the failing sun. He smiled. He was several years ahead of her if he was really who she was thinking of, a senior, class of '84, when she started her freshman year. She'd never spoken to him. He'd be twenty-two or -three now, but he looked as if he'd been traveling for a long time. The solitude and the dust of the miles had worn him. It was no longer the face of a cute teenage boy-man. It had become, she thought, one of the most startling faces she'd ever seen.

"Old Indian Bend High. There's a place you don't go around thinking about."

"I don't remember your name," she confessed. "I mean—we didn't know each other. I just remember— I'm Darcy."

"Will," he said. "Call me Will."

It didn't sound like the name of the boy she remembered.

Still without looking at her, he said, "It turns out that wherever you go in the world, of all the Americans you meet, half will be from Ohio. It's some kind of weird natural law."

"Is that true?"

He looked at her then, and she felt something shift and give way. Perhaps, it occurred to her, this was what she'd been waiting for.

"I don't know," he answered. "Do you believe it?"

"I don't know," she said. "I'm just really thirsty."

SOME TIME LATER, AFTER THEY'D eaten, they walked in the deep dusk north along the river.

"Where do you stay?" she asked him.

"At the Olympic Village."

"Ha-ha."

"They were here in '60."

"I knew that."

"And now one of the dorms is a hostel."

"Really?"

"It even has a bar. Just beer and wine, but what the hey."

She said she'd never heard of a hostel with a bar, but then she'd never actually stayed in one.

"Best party in Rome. You should come up. Get off the tour for a while. It's not very far from here."

"We leave in the morning."

"Then come tonight. I can at least buy you a couple beers."

"That sounds sooo good. But they— Mrs. Abignale got us all tickets to the opera. *Le Nozze di Figaro.*"

"Oh, that one."

She laughed. “I’d rather come with you,” she said. “I’d love to. A real birthday party.”

“So come.”

On Via della Conciliazione the traffic was dense and close, and the exhaust fumes did not smell like the exhaust fumes in other places. The crowds parted and rushed around them, and the air was so clear, the world so sharp, that she felt for a moment she could see her future in it.

Then the wine and the food and the fatigue swirled together. She tottered and gripped his arms. He put his hands on her sides to steady her, and when she rested her head against his shoulder, she could smell him, the mingled odors of sweat and wine and the faint remnants of something she could not identify, some strange boy scent. She could feel his wrists pressing against the lateral swell of her breasts.

She raised her face suddenly then and kissed him. When they kissed again, she put her arms around his neck and held on as if it meant something. She felt as if she were falling, with all the attendant dangers and fears, but she did not care. This was life. This was Europe. Not some dried-out corpse she was forced to pick over, but a real warmth. Life.

“Forget it,” she said so close to his ear that she could feel her breath against him.

“You’re not coming?”

“No. I mean the opera. Forget that.”

“Really?”

“Why not?”

He said, “Is it really your birthday?”

“Nineteen.”

“Ancient.”

"Me and Rome."

"You really want to come? It's not that far."

"I do. I should check in, though."

He looked disappointed now—as if this were her dodge, as if he were certain that once she got back into her warm room or the clutches of Mrs. Abignale, she would not come out again.

"I just—" She turned and pointed at the hotel. "I'd like to get cleaned up. Change and stuff."

"Sure," he said.

"I'd have to tell them, you know—"

"Right. Okay. Well—"

"Later, then?"

"Whatever. The invitation's open. I'll be there. Cab'll know where it is."

"You don't think I'm coming, do you?"

"No."

He almost looked relieved.

"Okay."

"Okay what?"

"We'll just see."

"I guess we will."

"Bye then. For now."

He smiled. She could feel him watching her run toward the soft, pretty light that spilled out between the heavy draperies of the lobby of the Hotel Abitazione.

MRS. ABIGNALE, WHO WAS FIVE-TWO and had an absurdly wide mouth and hair almost exactly the color of Mercurochrome, was by the front desk when Darcy went in. The woman had obviously been waiting there for her for some time and was as red in the face from perturbation as Darcy was from the eating and drinking and walking and kissing she'd done.

Mrs. Abignale almost jumped in the air. "Darcy," she said. "You just have time. They're still serving dinner . . ."

"I already ate," Darcy informed her.

Mrs. Abignale stopped for a full second, her great mouth dangling open, then recovered and said, "You have to get ready. We need to be on the bus in an hour. One hour." The opera. Just the thought of it made Darcy cramp. As she walked past, Mrs. Abignale added, "Please don't do this again."

"Do what?"

"It's my responsibility to keep track of everyone, and if you all decide to go wandering away . . ."

"All?"

"You."

Darcy said, "But I'm not your responsibility." She wasn't arguing, really. She didn't mean it to sound argumentative—just factual.

"You certainly are."

"I certainly . . ." Darcy felt her face grow even redder.

"Dear, no one's saying you can't go for a walk. But you're part of a group, and you just need to let me know where you are and when you'll be back. Basic courtesy."

"Miss?" It was the clerk behind the counter. He held a folded sheet of paper.

"Oh, yes, you got a call," said Mrs. Abignale as Darcy went over. "Your parents." When Darcy gave her a look of "How do you know that?" she hurried on. "I spoke with them. Or, rather, they asked to speak with me. They were concerned when no one knew where you were."

"And how are the old folks?"

"Fine, I take it. Darcy . . . they said they called to wish you a happy birthday. Why didn't you say anything? I could—"

"I didn't want to say anything. I just wanted to go for a walk."

"Well," Mrs. Abignale said, "all right then. Let's just hurry on."

In the room it was Rhonda's turn to bitch, but she just flounced at first, not speaking at all. She huffed and hummed and jammed some weird cookies into her mouth. If the girl would just limit it to meals, Darcy had thought when they first started rooming together, she'd drop fifty pounds in a month. Finally, when Rhonda was suitably fortified, she said, "So. Have fun?"

"I just went for a walk, Rhonda."

"For five hours?"

"And I had dinner."

"Alone?"

Darcy looked at her. "What'd you do?"

"Nothing. We went to these stupid caves, then just came back here. I think Abignale needed a nap."

"Why didn't you go out then?"

"I did. I went biscuit shopping."

DARCY HAD JUST GOTTEN OUT of the shower and was finishing toweling off before the mirror when the phone rang.

Rhonda said, "You know who that is. They've been calling all stupid afternoon."

Darcy wrapped a towel around her hair and answered on the fourth ring.

"Hi, Mommy. Daddy." Daddy wouldn't say much, but she knew he was there on the extension. She then held the phone a good foot away from her ear, at which distance her mother's voice, a high, nasally trumpet of a thing, was still easily audible, or at least certain of the more heavily stressed words were.

". . . were you?" Darcy heard.

She brought the phone to her mouth to speak. "I had a date. And I'm going out again. How about that? Pretty amazing, huh? And on my birthday."

Phone away. ". . . date?"

Phone in. "Someone I went to high school with."

". . . possible?"

"We just happened to run into each other and had dinner. He's asked me out tonight. . . . Yeah, he's on a tour, too. A hotel not far from this one."

". . . ticket . . . opera?"

"Well, I'm sure they can carry it off without me there."

". . . *paying* for this . . . *hate* Americans . . ."

"Yes, I know. I'm careful."

". . . responsi*bil*ity . . ."

"I can't hear you very well, Mommy. I'm meeting him at his hotel. I should really go. Thanks for calling!"

She set the phone down and finished drying her hair. Even with the rubbing of the towel she could hear the voice blaring on for at least a full minute before it was finally silenced.

Two

ON THE BRIDGE I PRACTICALLY warned her away from me, gave her every chance to realize her mistake, to smile and walk off, back into her life. But when it became clear she had no intention of doing that, I figured it wasn't really as if I were taking advantage. Some people just begged for it. Of course it occurred to me that maybe she hadn't made a mistake at all, that she knew I wasn't who she pretended to think I was. But I was far too hungry to think my way through all the possible wrinkles that suggested.

The trattoria I led her to was a real one, an honest neighborhood place not far from the bridge, with a trellised garden and the stuccoed building beyond it entombed by greenery, and the short, round, and so very Italian woman who greeted us in the courtyard with a wide dark-toothed smile and heavy open arms. It was perfect. I understood little of what the woman said. This girl, however, this Darcy, whoever she was, said something back to the woman in Italian—only a couple of words, but the woman laughed happily and waved us inside. And, oh, it was perfect, the smells so rich and thick they almost made me sick. It had been so long. And this Darcy got it, too, and went all goofy over it, and I, well, I didn't. I just kept it cool, watching her, but inside I felt as goofy as she acted. How weird that you could be standing there, starving, watching the river with nothing, no prospects, no chance, and all of a sudden here you were.

I sucked down all the good dark-crusted bread and then lifted the wicker basket and shook it, but the waiter pretended not to notice. It was only when Darcy said, "*Per favore, signore. Un,* uh, *un po' di più,*" that the ass hurried over, simpering and tipping his head, and took the empty basket away. When he brought more, I ate that, too, spread thickly with white butter, and it was so chewy fresh and good, I could've just had that and been satisfied. I felt the molecules breaking apart and moving into my body, filling my spaces, my cells, rebuilding me.

We'd been scrapping too long this time, and I could feel myself getting worn out by the hardness of it, the emptiness. There was something wrong with Justine. Always before, she managed things, she taught me, and we did well. We could take whatever we needed and live on it nicely, in whatever ways we chose, but now we were stuck.

I ate. I ate the salad and the mosticelli and the veal and yet more of the bread and a plate of fruit and tiramisu, and I could've eaten more, but this was fine. Darcy ate some, too, but mostly she drank and watched me. When she ordered a second bottle of the house Chianti, I took off my jacket, finally, and leaned back and felt my belly straining nicely at my shirt.

"When's the last time you ate?" she asked.

"Few days. It's been a little lean lately."

"Who's Bill?"

My shirt was one of those blue-and-white-striped jobs they wore in the service stations back home, with the name *Bill* embroidered on a red patch over the breast pocket. I couldn't even remember anymore where I picked it up.

"Yours," I said. "Thanks for asking." I laughed, expecting that she would, too. It was pretty funny if you think about it, a nice little joke on the whole situation, and humor was a big part of it after all. Or it should be anyway. The old give-and-take. But she didn't even smile, just kind of rolled her eyes.

"The truth is, I really am totally busted," I said. "But I'll pay you back. Seriously."

"When would you do that?"

"When—"

"I mean how? Will you track me down?"

I shrugged.

"Can I just buy you dinner?"

"Sure," I said. "Yes. Thank you."

She was with twenty or so other American students, she told me, on this very organized unspontaneous tour of the art and architecture of the Continent, six weeks, ten cities. Tomorrow it was on to Florence and then northward and westward, until they ended up in London. She'd gotten away this afternoon just by walking out of the hotel without telling anyone. She was in trouble. She'd hear about it when she got back.

I told her I was just a traveler. I'd been on the Continent over a year already and on the road for two. She seemed to get off on this, going all dreamy again and shaking her head as if she could hardly imagine it. And the truth was, she couldn't. She had no idea. So in exchange for a good meal I'd be her little slum-side experience, the rough edge that would pull all the beautiful crap she'd see into a new focus.

WHEN I GOT BACK, AS I passed the check-in desk and went into the hostel's dim foyer, three different people—a large-headed girl from Modesto, a German woman named Helena, and some guy from Boston I'd never seen before—all told me that Justine was waiting for me in the women's dorm. They all said it seriously, too, so I knew what to expect. I still wonder, when I remember it, at the fact that those strangers, those wanderers, some of whom had been there only a few days, did her bidding like that, treated her as if she mattered, as if she ran the place and they meant something to her. Even the people who worked there treated her that way. *La Madre,* they called her. Mother Justine.

I found her sitting on a bed, alone in the long room of bunks, and sensed that she had even arranged that. Before she looked up at me, I guessed the situation from the way her knees bounced, as if she were running somehow while still sitting. And when I saw her eyes, I was certain. Then I noticed the opened pill bottle on the blanket beside her and said, "How'd you manage this?"

"Nice to see you, too, love," she said in her smoothest, most beguiling Kentish, as she called it—a Canterbury upbringing polished by years in West London and America. Which is where I'd met her two years before as I sulked in a bar on my twentieth birthday. Later, when we'd been together for a while, I started asking her to take me to see where she was from, but she always refused, as if there was something there she didn't want me to see. Eventually I quit asking.

"How'd you get it?" I said.

"I bought it," she said, "with the last of what we had."

"Why?"

"I thought you'd enjoy it. I got something for us both. How was your day?"

"I thought we weren't going to. I thought we said we had to take a break."

"Well, we're at the end of it, aren't we? Our little adventure."

"Are we?"

"It seems we're in the process of the old crash and burn, doesn't it, Will? Rust never sleeps and all that. So I say let's burn out with it. Let's just play it out and sod all."

"And then what?"

"I have no idea, my sweet."

"Gimme some."

"Such a greedy monkey," she said, but she tossed the bottle farther down the mattress so that some of the pills spilled out. I picked out two and swallowed them dry.

"Does this mean we're leaving?"

"On what would we leave? You going to walk home?"

I sat, mulling on it, until she said, "Oh, stop the worrying. I'll get us out of it. I always have, haven't I?"

It was true.

"Hungry?" she said and began to reach into the canvas bag at her feet.

"I got dinner," I said. "A good one."

I told her briefly about the happy accident that led to my getting fed and thought she might at least be glad of it, that she didn't have to worry about my eating for a day or two. I thought she'd see the humor in how it was all the girl's doing, she who stopped and spoke to me, and how I didn't have to do anything but play along, turning things a little this way and that, how she even said she'd come out here later tonight, and who knew, maybe she would, but what the hell, it was all kind of funny. So I thought it might bring out a smile at least.

Justine said, "Well, aren't you the selfish bastard? You really believe she's coming here?"

"I don't know."

"Of course you do. You knew all along she wasn't coming out to a flipping youth hostel. Not after she sobers up. So you had your little fun, got your nosh-up, and old Justine can just piss off."

"What'd you want me to do? Bring a doggie bag?" I could have, I realized then. Ordered something else and brought it along.

Justine said, "Did you even try to get anything off her? Of course not. Because that would've helped me as well as you. But you don't think about that. You got your own belly filled, so why worry about the old hag?"

"Justine—"

"*I* don't think that way. I'm always thinking of you—how can I help *us*? How can I make it better for *both* of us? So I got us a little something to make it nice, you know? For *us.*" She slapped the mattress so that the pills and the bottle jumped. "I put myself through all of this to get something you'd appreciate. And not only haven't you said even a bloody thank-you, it turns out you were out getting yourself a nice belly full. And that's the end of that. I wonder—did you get a little something extra out of it, too?"

"Oh, God."

"No? Too bad. Because that would've been perfect, then, wouldn't it? The whole enchilada. You could've slept happily for days."

"I don't get you."

"Sod off, Will."

Which I did. I went back out and walked for a long time. I thought about just keeping on going. And then when I reached into my pocket and found I'd lost the stainless Clerc automatic I'd managed to slip off the arm of a smelly German tourist on the shuttle to the Saint Sebastian Catacombs just the week before, I howled and swore into the night. What I needed any of this grief for anymore I did not know, and although I finally felt that narcotic blanket wrap around me, and felt thirsty and as if things really could get better somehow, I still thought about the possibility of going off on my own.

I thought about it all the way back to the hostel.

LATER, IN THE BIG ROOM where the smoke rose into the lights, and people laughed and shouted over the jukebox, and the cold bottles of Czech Bud came one after another, I began to feel better. I was almost having an actual conversation with Didier—the Franglais we'd worked out becoming more comprehensible the more we drank—and I began to get back a little of the glow I had after dinner and hanging out with the pretty rich girl. A tour, she'd said. Six weeks. What kind of money, I wondered, must the daddy of someone like that have? A girl barely out of high school and bored already with the whole world, or at least the privileged part of it. She made it clear, though she didn't come right out and say it, that this tour thing was just about more than she could put up with. It was stifling the life out of her, and she'd really rather go off and drink at a cruddy hostel than go to the opera they had scheduled for that night. The opera, I thought as I drank in the cruddy hostel. What'd she know about any of it?

But I was glad, I decided, that she'd gone back to where she belonged. It would have been bad for her if she'd come with me, and I realized I didn't want it to be. At first, of course, I'd thought of her as prey. But then she wasn't. I had begun to like her already. I liked her ripeness, the sense that she was still unfolding, but at the same time I liked the acid she'd already learned to give off. I liked that burn.

We'd had a nice little thing, and now she was a nice memory, and that was the right thing for her to be.

I laughed at Didier, who grinned back because he was just a happy old drunk. I shook my head and looked around at the girls dancing together, at the guy letting his dog drink beer from a bowl, at the two American queens who'd come in last night arguing with each other and were still at it, and at all the people hanging on each other. My eyes rolled over it and past the entrance to the hallway, and on a little bit from there before they snapped back.

She was there. There she was. She'd come.

"Holy God," I said.

" 'O-lee *Gawd*!" said Didier.

I watched her for a moment—she hadn't seen me yet—then looked at Justine. She was at the bar, drinking and chatting with her bartender buddy and a couple of the older ladies who were always glomming on to her. I stared until Justine felt it and looked back. I tipped my head and glanced at the girl, Darcy, who was still standing there trying to figure out what to do with all this craziness, about as far from her world as I imagine she'd ever been. Justine raised her eyebrows. I nodded. She could only shake her head. It was pretty unbelievable that a mark would just walk into the den and offer herself up. And yet I felt it again: a little pause of regret. The vestige of the attraction I'd felt for her. But now it was too late, misgivings or not. Here she was with a reloaded purse and an open mouth and her big eyes and big chest and big hair, having no idea yet what she'd walked into, no clue that she was about to learn what it felt like to get fleeced and left out in the cold.

I put my fingers in my mouth and whistled. It rose over the din and caught her ear, and she looked directly at me. I stayed put, though. Didn't make a move toward her. It was for her to fight her way through the crowd. To come to me. To come in. To join the party.

"What'd you—have to pay?" I shouted. She carried the sleeping sack and pillowcase they give you when you check in. She nodded and flushed a little. At the hotel you could see she'd uncapped the hairspray and fired up the blow-dryer to get the maneish volume that was so in vogue then and that she wore so well.

I said, "Sorry about that."

"It's not a bad cover for the hottest club in town."

"There you go." I pointed toward Didier, of the glossy black beard and tied-back hair, and said, "Darcy, Didier. He's a carpenter from Montreal. He pretends he can't speak English so he can screw with my head."

She sat across from the older man and said with a perfect accent, "*Est-ce que cela lui fait une tête de baise?*"

Didier threw his face up, pounded the table, and laughed so hard I was afraid he was going to vomit.

"What?" I said. My French was nowhere near good enough to pick up her meaning.

"She wander do dis make you a fock head," said Didier.

"For sure," I told him.

"Fer shure," Didier mimicked, driving it through his nose.

"Beer?" I asked Darcy.

"Wine? White."

"You got it." I slipped into the crowd and left them to chat.

NOW, AT THE BAR, JUSTINE wouldn't look at me though I stood with my arm against hers. She said, "Pretty incredible, baby boy," in the accent that still sounded exotic to me even after these couple years.

Justine was a dark woman—hair, eyes, skin, soul—and she wore a yellow scarf around her throat tonight and a loose skirt with different-colored scarves hanging from it and a loosely knit sweater. She was thirty-nine years old.

What she was really saying now was "You were right. You win. So go ahead and gloat." But if I even hinted at vindication, Justine would use that as an excuse to start in all over again, crawl up my back. I figured her pleasure at seeing this girl here was just about evenly counterbalanced by her indignation at having been so vocally wrong. And it would take the tiniest tip to send the thing over again in that direction. So I said nothing.

"Well?" she said after several moments.

"She'll be good for it. We should do all right."

"I'm sure," she said.

She waited for me to offer some advice as to how to go

about it, but again I refused to bite. She was running it still. I acknowledged that. I didn't care. I just didn't want to get into it with her.

"She's having wine," I said finally. "I'll get a few down her." The implication was: Then you can take over.

Justine placed her palm on the back of my neck.

"Nice work, boyfriend," she said, and I knew I'd played it right. Made her happy again, at least for the moment. She looked at me now and smiled.

DIDIER WAS SAYING TO DARCY, "And so you just see him on da street, just like dat?"

"I guess that's right."

"Magic," he said. It sounded like *ma-zheek*. "Magic of the road. He say he hope you to come."

She smiled and looked up as I set the drinks down. She kept her eyes on me but said to Didier, "He told me he's been traveling here for a year."

"For me," Didier said, tapping himself on the chest, "more dan tree."

"How old are you?"

"Four-four," Didier said. "You sink my wife dat she missing me yet?" He laughed again then grabbed my arm and said, "Dis one, he a good man. He just here"—he tapped his own temple—*"un peu fou. Tu comprends?"*

A little nuts, he was saying. Which I granted. I had dropped out of college, after all, to run off with a woman I barely knew and done dangerous things—chemical, sexual, criminal—with her for which I'd had no previous desire or inclination. But in the years before I met Justine, I had failed to comprehend (or rather had forgotten) the power of imagining. I suppose that was her great gift to me. I was coming to recognize the malleability of reality itself. This story is in some part, I suppose, about my renaissance.

I slid a beer to Didier and the wine to Darcy, and lifted my own bottle. “To the opera,” I said, “that you’re not at.”

“Amen,” she said.

Three

THEY SHOT POOL. THE GIRL laughed and dropped her head whenever she made a stupid shot, and Will grinned and bumped her out of the way with his hip. Cute. She even got Will to dance when someone played "Psycho Killer." Justine had never seen him do that before. And, of course, they drank—they and the greasy idiot Didier in his lumberjack shirt. The girl had the silly tart act down pretty well, although she didn't look like someone who would let herself get too off her tits. But then assistance was available in that regard.

Young Gianfranco, the boy-bartender, brought another glass. Justine couldn't pay anymore, and wouldn't have in any case, and Gianfranco knew that. But it didn't matter. She was here. It was her temporary court. People came to talk, to stand by her, and when they ordered their own drinks, if they failed to offer to buy her one, too, Gianfranco simply deducted a little something extra from the bills they handed him. They never counted the change anyway.

They called her *La Madre.* They sought advice. They sought compassion. Revenge. Chemicals. Some of them didn't know what they sought, they just came to be near. And Justine smiled and nodded and let them touch her in their subtle ways. This was Rome, after all.

It wasn't hard to imagine Will watching the water slip beneath him, imagine him feeling he was watching time itself roll away, feeling himself getting older even as he stood there above the dirty old Tiber. Justine imagined him looking at the watch, fiddling with it, the Clerc he'd nicked a week earlier. He could have pawned it and fed them both for days, but he fell in love with it, a stupid boy trick, and now he was hungry.

She knew that hunger. Justine knew all the hungers. They would age anyone. Will was a child still, she often told him. "You're my little boy now, and I will take care of you, as a good mother should." But lately she had not. So it had come to this point, of the boy standing over the river, feeling that empty pain, watching the flow, and undoubtedly thinking about how it was no longer the Justine who'd rescued him. How that Justine had gone away somewhere, and how tired he was. Road tired, yes, and hunger tired, and not-enough-sex tired, and lonely tired—all of those, but those were understandable, to be expected. This was another kind of tired. A tired of. Tired of fighting. Tired of waiting. Tired of being tired.

Justine knew, and she knew that Will thought she did not. Will didn't believe Justine understood anything except herself. He had it just exactly backwards.

As he stood looking down, watching the flow, Justine could picture the young woman coming onto the bridge as clearly as if she had been there herself.

And now, however improbably, she, the wealthy little American wonder girl, was here—drinking, dancing, bumping, giggling, and watching Justine, even as Justine watched her. She caught the glances, the peeks in the direction of the bar. The girl might have been naive, but she wasn't stupid. She knew where the power lay. So it was time to move. Justine said *ciao* to Gianfranco and slid him a little change. When Will and the girl got back to their table, they found her sitting there, acting friendly with Didier, who by that time was so drunk he could barely speak.

"Well, hello," she said. "I'm Will's mother." The girl's eyes widened. Didier started to laugh, and Will laughed, and Justine smiled at her and said, "Sit, baby girl."

And just like that the girl was beside her, close to her, leaning in so that their arms brushed, as if the two of them were already fast friends or as if Justine was the one she had really come here to see. That was just how she was, how she felt to people—as if they could lean on her.

"So you found our little Will wandering the streets and bought him some dins."

The girl nodded.

"That was generous of you."

"Not at all."

"She say she knowing him," said Didier, seeming to wake up. "She say dey go to *l'ecole* togedder. Den she jus see him on da . . . *qu'est ce que s'avez dire, le pont?*"

"Bridge," the girl said.

"Ah, oui."

"Really," Justine said. "Kind of amazing, isn't it?"

The girl gave a sheepish little smile and looked away. It was all so much goofiness, but Justine understood how delicious it felt. She understood that. Everything, even the stupid parts, were so rich and filling.

"*Oui*, yes. Amazing," said Didier. "Ho-lee Gawd."

"But then lots of things are amazing," Justine said.

"What do you mean?" the girl asked.

"Just how it works out. How you want something, maybe, but you don't even know what it is exactly. You just know you want it. You want to find out what it is, and then you want to have it, but you have no idea how to go about it. And then it just comes to you. And there you are."

She could feel Will watching as the girl stared at her, as she fell into the black pool of Justine's eyes.

The girl said, "And what do I want?"

"You're asking me? I just met you."

"What do you want?" Will asked.

"I don't know. I know I have to go soon because I have to get up really early, like six, and take a bus to the train station and a train to Florence so I can see even more classic *merde* and follow the creep of Western civilization across Europe."

"But—"

"But what I really want is another drink."

Justine smiled and put her hand alongside the girl's on the table so that their pinkies overlapped. "Well," she said, "we can manage that. That's what we're here for."

SO JUSTINE AND THE GIRL had themselves a good old-fashioned chin-wag. And it struck her finally what the girl wanted. It was true what Will had said earlier—one like this, from money and all, having herself flown all over the world to study this or that, was bloody bored with it, hard as that might be to imagine. But that was not the heart of it. She wanted what many of them wanted but didn't know it: someone to tell her no. Just that. You can't have that. Can't go there. Can't see this. No, no, no. Justine doubted anyone had ever said it to her.

There and then it was not her place to fill the girl's needs, to satisfy her unacknowledged desires. Rather it was the other way around: She was there to help see to theirs. It was Will who had to be looked after, and this girl was simply another means.

Still, a different thought flickered through Justine's mind, of the darker possibilities this woman might present. The possibility of salvation for them all. It was too beguiling to imagine. And what it would require, what it would cost, was too frightening. It was altogether too much to contemplate. And anyway, she told herself, the possibilities of its actually playing out, even if she decided to try to turn it that way, were next to nil. So put it away, she told herself. There was no chance.

Justine went to the bar and ordered another round, which, as it happened, the girl had offered to pay for. Nice, that. Beers for Will and Didier, wine for herself and the girl. She made sure to push all the change back at Gianfranco, who gave a wink as he set down the tray and said, "*Grazie, Madre.*"

She put her hand over one of the wineglasses and held it there for several moments, until the sudden fizzing and bubbling stopped.

The girl had mentioned the early train to Florence she had to be on with her group. That suggested possibilities. And those brought Justine back again to the dark notions brewing in her. She could see it laid out, the way it might play if she steered it just so, how it could end up being more than just the folding in the girl's wallet and a few pieces of plastic to fence. So much more. But that was a very different game, one she had forsworn when she found Will again.

Back at the table, the girl touched her on the shoulder and leaned in so close that she could feel her breathing.

"I've got to get up early."

"Not to worry," Justine whispered.

"One more," said Will. He leaned across and said something into her ear. The girl giggled and maybe even blushed a little. He was turning into a real pro, there was no doubt. But Justine couldn't help the jealous bite that came with watching it, the feeling that Will was enjoying this in ways that weren't strictly part of the game.

She handed out the beers and set one of the wineglasses in front of the girl, who said, "Oh, gosh."

"One for the road, sweet," Justine said. "Come on then, tip it up."

She sipped again, and Justine could see that she was on the edge anyway, that point where, if she were to let it go, she'd just keep drinking until she was stupid. But Justine also saw that the girl knew that. She had gotten good at getting very close without slipping over. Well, this would be something new for her then.

She took another sip. She knew where she was. That was why her first reaction, upon standing to go to the bathroom, was more surprise than anything. She looked as if someone had just hit her across the back of the knees with a cricket bat. They let go, and she caught herself on the table. The crowd around them let go a loud whoop in honor of someone else who couldn't handle the plonk, didn't know how to control herself. But it wasn't that, she seemed to want to tell them. It wasn't that, Justine almost wanted to say to her, to assuage her.

The girl sat for perhaps a full minute, watching. She took another sip. I'm okay, her face said. Okay. She stood again. And then, as if that invisible someone had moved the target higher, the bat came down across the back of her head this time. Justine could see the room swimming and swirling in her eyes. For a moment she panicked and seemed to struggle to draw breath. She opened her mouth and looked at Justine, who thought that in her own eyes the girl could perhaps see what it was. Justine saw, for just an instant, a realization, a dawning. The girl felt frightened, but that moment passed. It became an abstraction, a distant part of something else that was not now and not here. The crowd shouted again, but Justine did not think she heard it. Or, rather, she probably did hear it but would not remember, and so it would be as if it had never happened.

Now the girl no longer struggled to breathe. It was all that was left for her—breathing and looking blankly at the world and at Justine before her. *La Madre.* Always there to help.

Venice

Four

IN THE END, THE HARDEST part was just the making up of her mind—stepping back into an evil she had abandoned when she rediscovered Will. It was an enterprise she'd sworn off, though it had paid her well for years. And yet, she found, the opportunity was so perfect, so laid out, so irresistible that the decision had already made itself. There was nothing difficult about it after all. The whole thing seemed to have been fated. She barely had to do anything beyond simply setting it in motion.

After the GHB had kicked in and the girl went all vacant, Justine led her to a cot in an empty women's dorm and posted Will in the doorway to make sure it stayed that way.

He said, "What the hell?"

"What the hell what?"

"You had to do this?"

"What're you talking about? You brought her in. You did well, Will. I take it all back, what I said earlier. You are learning. Developing a sense."

As she spoke, she was already in the wallet. She plucked out a nice fat wad composed mostly of liras and American dollars, with some emergency deutsche marks and francs mixed in. The wallet wad was more than she had even expected.

"You couldn't've just lifted it?" he said. "You had to knock her out?"

"She's not out."

The girl was looking at them. Just looking. No expression.

When Justine put the wallet back, Will said, "She doesn't have any cards?"

"AmEx, Diners Club, and two Visas."

"Well?"

"I don't know. I have an idea."

"Oh, tell. Please."

"Don't be nasty. Think about it. Fencing plastic is a one-time shot, and a pretty small one at that. No? You've done it enough to know that. Even if you're stupid enough to use the bloody things, you can only do that a couple of quick times."

"What's your point?"

"Cards are worth much more attached to their rightful owner."

"What?"

"Besides," she added, "it's not going to break your heart to have her along for a bit of a ride, is it? You can't bear looking at her for a few more days?"

"Whatever," he said. "You still didn't need to do this."

"You like her, don't you?"

"What?"

"You're feeling protective. You care."

"Justine—"

"Maybe I should slip out and leave you two alone for a little while?"

"What?"

"She won't complain."

He looked at her a moment, then said, "That's sick."

"Oh, come on, baby. I understand. It wouldn't mean anything."

"Justine," he said, "stop it."

She undid the girl's blouse and removed it, and slipped off the jeans. Will stepped into the room, closer.

"It's some body she has," Justine said. She had a sudden image of herself pulling down the bra and squeezing one of those great charlies until it was long and pointed.

"Justine," said Will.

"So leave," she told him.

He did not leave.

"You know you're gagging for it."

"Please stop."

She looked at him, at the hurt on him, the confusion. Where was the jealous bitchy control freak he'd grown accustomed to? In the past she had spanked him for as much as looking at another woman's behind.

"Well," she said, "good for you. You not only bring us back some nice pickings but exercise admirable restraint and honor on top of it. I must've raised you right." She laughed at his scowling and then covered the girl, stood up, and put her hand on his trousers.

"I'm sorry it's been so long," she said. "This hasn't been the place for it. But I've been remiss. I haven't been myself—"

"Justine—" he said, though he barely had the breath for it.

"Shall we find a private spot somewhere?"

He breathed again and nodded.

WHEN THE GIRL STUMBLED INTO the great room, which in the new morning had transformed itself from a rocking club into a plain bland cafeteria, Justine was sitting with Will. Justine leaped up and went over to take the girl's arm and help her sit.

"Poor little pussy," she said.

After the girl took a few sips of the coffee Will had fetched her, Justine said, "Well, that was some pisser you put on, girlfriend. Bet your head's banging."

"It isn't," she said. "I didn't drink that much."

"Right," Justine said.

"I really didn't," she insisted. "Not for something like that to happen." She drank some more of the thick coffee and then said, "What did happen?"

"You got blitzed," Will told her.

"You just went over," said Justine, "like you were bloody knackered. I put you to bed."

"Thank you."

"So you feel all right now?"

"I'm okay. I just . . . Oh, no. Oh, *merde!*"

"What is it?"

"My bus. We're leaving. What time is it?"

"A bit after eight."

"Oh, my God, you're kidding. You're kidding, right?"

"No, dear. When did you say it leaves?"

"Left," she said. "Already. The bus was at seven. We had a seven-forty train."

"Well," said Justine, "don't get all wobbly. You should call the hotel. I'd guess someone stayed behind. They may even have called in the police. Where did you tell them you were going?"

"I didn't. I snuck out."

"That's brilliant. But I'm sure they're all waiting for you, worried sick."

"I don't think so. Mrs. Abignale is always saying, you know, 'If you can't be on time, you get left behind.' "

"They always say that, don't they? But they never do. Not really."

"You don't know her."

"You have the number? The hotel?"

She lifted her purse and had begun to root through it when she made another nasty discovery.

"Oh!" she said again. "My money's gone."

"It can't be," Justine said.

"It is. Someone stole it. I had a lot of cash."

"Lowlifes," said Will. "You can't believe the trash that hangs out in these kinds of places."

Justine said, "What're you going to do, dear?"

"I don't have any idea. I'm so screwed. I'm in so much trouble."

"What trouble? It's *your* bloody trip. It's not like you're a schoolgirl or something."

The girl looked at her then, and Justine could see it dawn on her that this was so. She was as free as any other adult.

"Of course," Justine continued, "the thing to do really is call. Let them know so they can collect you. Unless . . ."

She let it hang there between them until the girl said, "What?"

"I don't know. It's— I'm sure they'll want to just pick you up or something."

"Unless what?"

"Well, we could ride you up."

"You have a car?"

"No. Afraid not. I meant by train. We're checking out today anyway. Heading north. Getting on with things."

"You're going to Florence?"

"Well, we could do. We're sort of headed in that direction. The problem is we don't actually have enough money for tickets quite yet. There's a place we can give blood plasma, which should be enough."

"That's disgusting."

"No. It's all right."

"But what were you saying? About me?"

Justine shrugged. "We know our way 'round pretty well. We could just take you there, make sure you meet up with your group, find the hotel and all that. We could leave this morning except, well, we're all three of us flipping potless, aren't we?"

The girl looked at her, not understanding at first. Then the bulb went on. "No," she said. "Oh, no. I can get it. God. It's not that."

"I'm afraid you'd have to buy all three tickets."

"I don't care."

"I don't know. I'm sure they'll want to send someone round."

" 'They' being whom?"

Who Justine thought, and glanced at Will. "I'm sure I wouldn't know."

The girl said, "I'd rather just go with you guys."

"Rock 'n' roll," said Will.

"First," Justine said, "you really will have to call someone. Let them know you're alive. I don't want the police coming after us for kidnapping or something. And then you'll have to go round and collect your luggage. You'll—We'll need a taxi."

"First," the girl said, "I have to find an American Express."

"Ah. Right. Well, believe it or not, I know where one is. Not far from here, really."

"Will you take me?"

"Will can. You know where it is?"

He said, "Sure."

"I really must finish my own packing."

"We'll get a cab then and come back for you," the girl said.

"Wonderful," said Justine. "That sounds really perfect."

In the end, after Darcy had wadded up again courtesy of AmEx, and after a wine-soaked lunch (on that same lovely gold card), and after getting her packed up and out of the hotel (where, Justine discovered, someone from the tour had in fact been waiting until Darcy called), and a few last-minute errands that mostly involved seeing some people and settling some things, it took the entire day to finally get to the station, and then they had to hustle. This was, of course, by design. They had made sure they arrived moments before the train was to leave. So they ran, the girl between them, explaining to her that they didn't have to buy tickets in the station. They could just pay the conductor when he came around. They made the platform just as the doors were beginning to close. Darcy tried to stop and ask a question, but they hurried her on board, somehow found an empty set of facing seats, and collapsed into them.

They were half an hour out of Rome when the announcements came over the tinny speaker. Justine could see the girl listening. It was hard to make out, but she did because she looked at them and said, "We're on the wrong train."

"What?"

"We're going to Venice."

"No," Justine said. "Florence. I'm sure of it."

"We got on the wrong stupid train."

"You're mistaken."

"I am not."

She put on a good rich-girl look of pissiness and aggravation then, a look of "What have you cock-ups done now?" But when she turned toward the window to watch the last light fading on the ancient hills with their ancient vines, Justine could have sworn she saw a thrill in the girl's face, a smile she tried to hide. Like when you feel that little tingle on a fast lift as the floor drops away and you hang there, just for an instant, in midair.

So now it was *La Serenissima,* city of canals, on the morning after they walked over the bridge from the Santa Lucia Station into a fog so dense they could hardly see one another, and so late that nothing was open. They stood, stupidly looking around, as figures emerged and vanished again around them. They would have slept shivering on benches except that Justine knew where to go, a nice place where she had stayed once. Small and quiet. Locanda Apostoli. Not someplace she could afford anymore, but she knew the girl was good for it. She'd had it in mind that they would get two rooms, one for her and Will, but the girl surprised her by flat-out refusing. Justine said nothing. She wasn't even angry, just a bit gobsmacked. The girl had refused nothing up to that point. But it was late by then, and she was whacked and cranky. She said one room was enough for them just to crash in, and so they did. They fell onto the bed in their clothes and slept that way, touching, Justine to Will, and Will to her.

Justine was up early because she had business—real business at last. The two children still slept.

She watched as a cross on the top of a low white church across a canal began to blush and shine, as if it were giving off its own light, as if it were a holy rapturous thing. She watched the rooftops become orange and alive. The water of that place began to twinkle as the new light made its way into the shadows.

She had to see Maurice, much as she hated the thought, much as it made her stomach twist and ache. She had begun this job, or it had fallen to her like some gift, some low fruit waiting to be plucked. And it would solve their problems—that was the real point. That was what she had to keep in mind. It would make them flush again, even more than flush. And they owed Maurice so much besides. A couple of thousand. It would wash that all away. There was nothing for it now but that. Him.

In the beginning, after she'd found Will, she cared so much. She made it nice. She taught him how to run the scams and cons that fed them and kept them. It was fun, her teaching and him learning, and they made a packet. America first and then Europe were like playgrounds again in ways they had not been to her for a long time. They were new to her through his eyes.

Then Maurice found her again. Found them. They were in Amsterdam, where Will had already grown partial to the hash bars. He liked that pipe. But after Maurice came, he got to try everything, and he was soon drawn to darker pipes. Opium. Sometimes he and Maurice would smoke it for days. Justine was not that type. She always needed to feel the edge, not dull it. She liked it fast and bright, so she was partial to meth. She was an old speed freak, actually, and had been on and off since she was thirteen. But she went off it when she found Will again and he came with her. She didn't need it. The world was plenty fast and bright.

Then, after Maurice came, after Will fell in love with the pipe, it began to change. She told Will it was a nipple, a mother's tit. She might touch him and pull out her own and let him go back and forth, one tit to another, hers to the pipe. She watched him that way until her nipple got as hard as the mouthpiece, and Will grew so simultaneously high and turned on that the confusion itself became a kind of drug, and he did not know what he wanted most in the world, to sleep or to shag. She knew. What he wanted most was that in itself, the confusion, the pain of it. It was what she gave him.

SHE WORKED ON THE FAG Maurice gave her. She hadn't wanted to take it off him, but she had needed it, the more they talked. She knew the less she said the better off she'd be, so she smoked as hard as she could, as hard as she wanted a piece of some big action, as hard as she needed this job to break right for her and Will—to get them out of this hole they'd fallen in.

She and Maurice were in a cramped little back room of a middling hotel. It was a storage closet of mops and buckets and steel racks, of sheets and blankets, a weird sort of office, but Maurice used it whenever he was in Venice. He knew the hotel owner—in fact, the owner owed him money. Maurice said it was so much that he basically owned a piece of the place himself. Of course he stayed here free. But instead of his room to meet in, he used the janitor's closet. He had learned to be careful that way. Rooms had ears. Closets never did.

He sat on a turned-over bucket and watched Justine. He said how she was going to suck the filter off if she wasn't careful. She ignored him. He put on the pissy look he often got. She hated it. But she hated it worse when he said things like "You can't even afford 'em anymore, can you?" Meaning cigs.

Still, she said nothing. He pressed again about whether she was really interested in doing this. In coming back. Because if he set it in motion, he couldn't put it back. It involved other people, and they weren't the sorts to be trifled with.

She looked at the ash and then took another drag.

And was she finally ready to pay back the two K she owed him? Wouldn't that be nice? Was she finally sick of the Mickey Mouse scams she and the boy did? He didn't get how they could live like that. The penny ante. He just didn't see the point.

And oh, she thought, wasn't that the very truth itself? He did not get it.

She had known it was coming, this nattering. This "I told you so." She'd known and prepared herself for it, but it didn't make it any better. It was like knowing you were going to vomit. It was just as awful when it came whether you knew or not. Still, she could hold on to what would come after. How it would be.

But when he took a plastic baggie from his pocket, she could see straight off what was in it: blacks for her and reds for Will. She imagined that this bleeding bloater, this sodding shit to whom it happened she was once upon a time duly and legally wed, could hear the increase in her pulse.

He set the bag on the floor beside his bucket and pointedly offered her nothing from it. It was meant to lie there within her sight, hers to keep if she played nice. She dragged and exhaled. Maurice looked like a nothing, a nobody. Pulpy nose. Heavy brows above his eyes and blue bags beneath. Thin in the lips. Short neck, short body. A kind of bread loaf of a person. And he had the crude East End idiom to go with it. But he was not nothing, and he hadn't always looked this way. He'd been thinner when they were together, more angular and piercing. When he started in about the money again, she closed her eyes and smoked.

"A naffin' youth hostel," he said. "That's what I heard. Someone your age." He laughed.

"We're at Locanda Apostoli now," she told him. They'd stayed there together once.

"Well," he said, "aren't we the sudden nob."

She drew so hard on the smoke that she felt the heat in the filter.

"So you must be using the boy for something other than begging coins," he said. "You renting him out? I bet there's some good cash in that."

She was afraid now of how it might turn out, and it made her feel bad. Though Will didn't see it, she was constantly aware of how hard it was for them then, how unsatisfied he was, how hungry, how ready to move on to fuller days, richer scenes. She could see it all. But it was as if she were frozen in something. As if even her fingers could not lift themselves. As if she had been swimming in a pool of glue, clear as the day but so thick that every movement required a conscious and extraordinary effort.

She looked Maurice in his sunken little eyes and said, "We need this, and it's a good deal. You'll see."

For a moment it looked as if there was ice forming in his eyes, over his retinas, or like cartoon steam was going to come out of his ears. Then he smirked.

"Maybe it is and maybe it isn't, Justine," he said. "But it's *you* that worries me. Just because you're gasping for it doesn't mean you're any good for this anymore. It's no small thing, as you well know. And we can't afford any cock-ups, neither of us. This is a hot customer, the big time. And the timing matters. It has to be on the island and delivered by Christmas, a special gift for someone who has everything. So I ask myself about you, 'Does she still got it?'"

It was the sunshine she thought of now, more even than the money. How long since she'd been down there? And how much would Will love it? She thought of floating, of salt water, of heat, and of resting for a long, long time.

"So I dunno. I got a bad feeling. You going after that boy again after all these years, like he was yours in the beginning."

"He was mine."

"He wasn't yours. He was just some flippin' squallin' brat. And I'm sure he still is."

"Four months, Maurice."

"I know how old he was. I was about."

"That's a long time for a baby. I helped form him, if you think about it, so he was mine. Part of him anyway."

"This is exactly what I mean. I'm sure you've cut his balls since you got him back, but it's like he's cut yours, too."

Now she felt the ice forming in her own eyes.

Maurice said, "If I decide to go ahead, I'll see you tonight. If not . . . then not."

Crete, she thought.

The cigarette was about finished, but she dragged hard on it once more so that it cooked right down, so the filter itself started to burn. She planted it between her lips, squinted, leaned over, and took Maurice's right hand in both of hers. She ran a fingernail across the palm. He watched stupid-eyed, the way he had always watched as she prepared to hurt him. She said, "How's this for cut balls, Maurice?" She took the burning dimp from her mouth and pressed the tip into the exact spot where his life line ended.

He screamed like an animal. He slapped at it and spit on it and ran to the utility sink.

She grabbed the baggie from the floor, opened the door, and stepped out into the less stale air of the hallway. Maurice was screaming at her and trying to get the water turned on. "Whore!" Time was that was one of her pet names for him.

She made sure to walk away slowly so he would not think her heart was beating as hard as it was. So he would not see how badly she needed this but how even now, flat broke and sick with desperation, she'd starve before she let some lowlife donk of an ex-hubby push her around. So he could not tell how badly she wanted to be away from him.

She walked slowly even when another door in the hallway opened and a very large man came out holding a handgun, holding it with both of his hands pointed floorward, as if he knew exactly what he was doing with it. She was sure he did. And when he aimed at her, she slowed even more. She nearly stopped. She looked at the man and could see in his eyes that there was nothing, that he was already as dead as he was planning on making her. She could feel his trigger finger begin to flex.

"No," Maurice said then from the doorway of his closet office. He held a wet coral-colored towel against his palm. "Don't."

She looked at him now. She stood with her hand on the handle of the outside door at the back of the hotel and looked at them both.

"Karl, don't," Maurice said again, although the man had already lowered the pistol and was fitting it into the holster that hung under his arm.

Maurice raised his own hands with the pinkish towel between them and aimed a finger at her. "You half-ass this one, Justine, and something might just have to happen to your pretty boy. Remember that."

She could only think of how badly she wanted just to lie down.

WALKING BACK TO THE LOCANDA, Justine felt as if someone had planted a fist inside her chest where the heart lived or as if she'd swallowed something and it had stuck there. She needed another smoke, but her pockets were empty. She had hidden the money she stole from Darcy and in her nervousness stupidly forgot to take some out this morning—and, besides, nothing seemed to be open yet. She watched the few passersby for a smoker she might bum one from, but saw none. The two dexies she'd swallowed dry from the baggie were kicking in already. The world flew and flashed, and she could hear the hum of the engines that turned it all down deep beneath the mantle. A gondola slipped past, and it was so perfectly gorgeous, so stupidly, postcardishly, touristically, romantically, sentimentally, momentarily beautiful that she nearly stopped and sat down at a table alongside a café just to watch it. But of course she didn't. She couldn't sit. She needed a cig so bad she thought she was going to retch.

IN THE ROOM SHE FOUND them still in bed. She dug into her pack and slipped some bills from the roll she'd buried there. She was about to rush back out to find an open fag vendor when she saw with a start that the girl was watching her.

"Hey," she said, all groggy-sounding, and then yawned.

Justine sat in the chair by the window. The cross was not glowing anymore. Her knees bounced again. She needed to go, but she found sitting nice, too.

Will sat up then and looked at her and said, "He gave you more?"

Such an observant little boy.

"Who?" said the Darcy girl. "What?"

"Road candy," he told her.

She didn't get it or pretended not to, but she crawled across the bed, giving Justine a perfect shot of her tight little posterior clad only in white French-cut knickers, the sort that pulled themselves up and right in there so you had to go around discreetly fingering them out every so often, so that Justine could all but see right up that charming little cunny. The girl went into the loo.

Little Bitch, Justine decided. That was her real name, or it would be if Justine had anything to say about it. Of course she didn't, wouldn't. But she found something about the girl appealing. Perhaps it was the skin of her face. How nice it would be to lick it. Or the slight fattiness of her bum. How Justine wanted to bite it. Or the shape of her breasts. What a thrill it was to think of binding them. But Justine thought that really it was the look she had sometimes. The look that something as shoddy and common as a pisshole hostel could be fascinating. It was as if the girl had stumbled into the Neverland or Alice's rabbit hole. As if some new and wondrous world had opened to her. She had this look, a most unjaded expression for a person of her status who was clearly trained in the projection of a veneer of sophistication. This smile. This wonder.

When Will had returned to the hostel after his little snit and Justine cooled down, they talked about what had happened that afternoon. He mentioned this about the girl: that when he got her to take him out to eat, it all seemed so fabulous to her. His word, delivered a bit dismissively, so world-wearily. What he didn't seem to realize was that he had the same look, the same wonder. Justine saw that about him straight off when she'd found him again two years earlier. He acted as hard and as bored in his way as this girl did, but he couldn't help the look that came over him sometimes, just as she could not. They were a pair in that regard.

The two wonder kids: Lick-lick and Little Bitch.

Anyway, it hardly bore thinking about.

"What did he say?" said Will.

Justine shrugged. "Might have a job."

"Really?"

"Be nice to make some cash, no?"

"God, yes," he said. "Doing what?"

She shook her head.

When the girl came back out, she grabbed her purse, an enormous shoulder bag that looked as if it was made from an old tapestry, and rifled through it—checking, Justine supposed, to see if any of her new money was missing. It was not. They'd milk this cow slowly now. But then when she tossed the thing to the floor, Justine saw, wonder of flipping wonders, what looked for all the world like a packet of coffin nails sticking out the top.

"You smoke?"

The girl shook her head.

"What is that?"

"Oh," she said, lifting the purse again and drawing out a gold and crimson pack of English Dunhills. "I picked them up somewhere. I don't know why."

"Would you mind?" Justine said, doing all she could to stay the shaking in her hands. Little Bitch shrugged and tossed the pack on the bed.

"Keep 'em," she said.

"You wouldn't happen to have—"

She reached in again and came up with a beautiful gold and silver lighter, a strangely expensive thing for a nonsmoker to carry. But all Justine could think was "Oh, God."

"Oh, God," she said. The girl gave her a little smirk. Justine opened the window, leaned out so as not to pollute the room too badly, and hung there in Venice, inhaling the wonderful poisons.

Behind her the girl said, "I'm hungry. Where can we get some breakfast?"

"Aren't you leaving soon?" Justine asked her.

"I should," she said.

"Because I was thinking," said Justine, "we could get some wine instead and some real food and have a picnic."

"Seriously?" said Will.

"Yes!" said Darcy.

She told the girl they could then take her to the station if she wanted. "I'm sorry about all this," she added.

"Oh," the girl said, all disappointed at being reminded that she had a life. "Never mind. It's fun. A picnic. In Venice."

It was amazing, Justine thought. Even when she offered to derail the thing, it just kept coming around. Here they were. Maurice would meet them tonight. It was happening.

The girl ran back into the bath then for a quick wash up so she could get dressed. Will, who was still under the sheets, could only shake his head in wonder.

Five

THE WORLD TOOK CARE. ONE time, after another fight with my parents, I managed to thumb clear up to Philadelphia. Along the way one of the rides I got, a middle-aged guy in a cheap tie, bought me lunch and a beer. When I thanked him later, he said just that: "The world'll take care of you, kid. You just gotta let it." It was only weeks later that I met Justine and my real education began—in letting the world take care, yes, but more than that: in making it, bending it, creating it as I went along.

That first full afternoon with Darcy in Venice we sat on a quay that was nothing more than a raised concrete slab, a utilitarian place where I imagined supply boats tied up to load or unload in the white December sun, in the glorious glorious heat of that reflected Venetian light. We had a hard loaf of bread, a brick of some strong cheese, and three bottles of cheap *vino da tavola*. I was riding on my bennies, Justine was quivering on her meth, and Darcy was just tripping on the whole world that was not the world she was supposed to be in—hanging out, unknown, unseen, unrecorded, on some hot concrete alongside a canal.

"Dang," she said, "this is amazing. This is *amazing*, Will."

I nodded at her and smiled but could not raise the gumption to make words.

"I mean what? Two days ago you're standing on a bridge, I'm on an art tour, and now here we sit."

Justine was watching her, almost smiling. "You grooving on it, little girl?"

"Totally," she said.

"It's all cool."

Justine talked about Crete then. At first I didn't understand why she was going on about it, but it dawned on me that we were going there. She'd seen Maurice, and something had come of that. I didn't know exactly what Maurice's business was, nor did I really want to. I knew that Justine had been involved in it once upon a time but hadn't been at least since I'd known her.

"It's warm. There are long beaches, and it's so cheap you can't believe it. Huge seafood dinners for a quid or two. Get yourself drunk as a lord for change. Rooms cost nothing. And plenty of others show up there as well—Americans, English, Aussies. It'll be a big Christmas bash, the whole place. And you've never seen a sky like that."

I'd never been, though we'd talked about it. It was a long way to Greece, and longer still out to the middle of the ocean. It would cost some money to get there, so we were surely not going just for the sun or the beaches or the Christmas parties. But, still, we were going. It warmed me simply thinking about it, and it warmed me more that Justine somehow had come back, in these past couple of days, from the edge of the abyss over which she'd been perched. She had not thrown herself off but had rallied, had responded to my good work, my bringing in of the girl, and had made it work for us, had made herself work on the work she did, which was to use other people for her own gain. And now we were off to Crete.

WE TOOK A NAP IN the afternoon, the three of us again lined up front to back on the smallish bed, as we had slept the night before—Justine facing me and me facing Darcy. But it was different now. Justine was wired for one thing and couldn't really sleep. She kind of dozed, but it was so shallow that she shifted constantly, talking to herself, making noises in her throat, moving her feet so that you knew she was in a running dream somewhere. Her hands played against my back. The first couple of times I looked at her, but she lay with her eyes closed, apparently unaware as she had seemed unaware of so much that happened between us.

She was a sadist by nature, Justine was. What she enjoyed in sex was being in control, whether that meant inflicting pain or bondage or just giving orders. I was not then particularly inclined to submissiveness, nor am I now, but I had learned to play that role with her. I did not find that it enhanced the experience, as I imagine true subs or masochists do, but it did change it and perhaps intensified it in some ways. For Justine, though, without playing the role of the controller, the inflictor, the web spinner, sex was flat. Enjoyable, perhaps, but in the way, say, a back rub is enjoyable. It held no spark for her.

The nap was different with Darcy, too, not because of how she slept but because of how we had awakened that morning.

Justine was gone; she had been gone for some time, I thought, though her early rising hadn't awakened me. When I opened my eyes, I found Darcy awake already and lying with her face near mine, looking at me.

"Hi," she said.

She touched my face and then turned over and pressed her back into me. We'd started out the night clothed and on top of the bed covers but at some point crawled underneath, and when she did, she took off her jeans so that all I felt when I touched her was the skin of her legs and the thin strap of her panties. Now she moved against me so earnestly that for a moment, as I was still coming awake, I was certain it was a dream. I put a hand on her hip and pressed back into her, moving now with her rhythm.

"Touch me," she said. I fumbled with her panties. She said, "Hurry."

I slipped my fingers under the thin fabric and into her, and she said, "Ah!" and proceeded, apparently, to have the most immediate female orgasm I'd ever been privy to.

She had just turned back toward me and unbuttoned my jeans when I heard the door and pushed myself away, far enough that we weren't touching, and lay still. Justine came in, and after a moment Darcy seemed to wake. She stretched and yawned and greeted Justine, and greeted me, too—"Good morning, Will"—as if nothing had gone on. And later, as I waited for some sign of what had transpired between us, a hint even, a touch, a look, a certain smile, I saw none.

Now, lying against her again, with Justine pressing into me from behind, sandwiched between these two women, one of whom I'd been with many times and the other whom I had just begun with, I felt that aching again of desire and frustration. I was certain I could never sleep like this, but the pills and the wine and the fatigue that always came with the road won over at last.

THE AMERICAN CAFÉ WAS A re-creation of an idealized U.S. diner complete with bottles of French's mustard and Heinz catsup on every table, Miller High Life in tapered clear-glass bottles, waitresses in short skirts and bobby socks, and a menu heavy with Ham Burgers and Shakes of Milk. I found it laughable that the people who came here were nearly all Americans, an odd mixture of tourists and those who'd been around Venice long enough to recognize one another. What did it mean? Were they homesick? Was this really like any place they ate at home? (It was rather startling, I have to admit, to see those neon yellow bottles of homogenized mustard we grew up with.) Did they come to Italy not wanting to eat the fabulous food, or did they find on arriving that, although its reputation preceded it, they just didn't like it? Couldn't they stomach it? Or did they need a break from it? Was it too good for their systems, and they had to pollute themselves to feel whole again? Was it akin to dropping into a McDonald's in Paris just to compare? And, by extension, did Italian visitors to the United States go out for pizza?

I didn't know. I just laughed at the diners around me in their logo-T-shirt-clad bellies and jeans and tennis shoes. Then I thought: Here I was, too. One of them.

Except not. Justine and I came here when we were in Venice for one reason, and it wasn't burgers. It was to see the man, Maurice, the one person to whom I had ever seen Justine pay anything resembling homage, though no one else who saw it would call it that. But he clearly held something over her, which I assumed at first was just about chemicals, about his being our supplier—until I found out they'd been married. I realized you could see it still between them, that uncuttable tie, that ghost of fealty, a vestige of which must always be there between former spouses—some remnant of the crazy love or whatever else it was that had drawn them together in that way. She looked up to him, that's what it was, and it was just plain weird to see, because she was a woman who looked up to no one.

We sat at a corner table, me and Justine on one side, Darcy across from us, watching the Americans and drinking Miller drafts and smoking what remained of Darcy's Dunhills. And then, as if he had simply materialized, Maurice pulled out the empty chair and sat.

"Heya," he said. He was wearing a loose-fitting lime-colored sport coat, black T-shirt and jeans, and high-tops, and he carried a gym bag in his right hand. His left was wrapped in a gauze bandage. He let his gaze rest for a particularly long moment on Darcy but said nothing.

"What'd you do?" I asked, nodding at the bandage, but got only a kick from Justine as an answer.

Maurice was quiet, then said, "So here we are." He was looking at me when he said this, but I wasn't the one being spoken to.

"We are indeed," Justine said.

"Well, I think things look fine. Just fine."

"Good."

"And you?"

"I'm well," Justine said.

"Bloody fantastic then," he said. "I knew you would be. I always know."

"You think you do," Justine said, and she seemed to drag rather vehemently at her Dunhill.

Maurice shook his head at me. "How d'you put up with her, Will?"

I shrugged and felt my face warm.

"You must be getting something good, or else she's just too flippin' much trouble."

"This is Darcy," Justine said.

Maurice looked at the girl again. He reached over and put his hand on her head, as if she were a small child, petted her hair, and said, "Lovely."

"We picked her up in Rome. Sort of an accident. She's supposed to be off to Florence tomorrow."

"Florence? What the fuck's there?"

"Art," Darcy said and looked away, out the window.

"Art?" Maurice said. "Coo, there's art everywhere over here. It's like litter. Justine said she thought you rather enjoyed her company and Will's."

"I do."

"Want my advice? Then keep it. It's the bloody Continent, you know? Do what the fuck you like. Be happy." He looked at Justine and said, "That's what I do, in'it?"

Darcy smiled at him rather genuinely. Maurice just laid it out there. Said what was on everyone's mind.

"Well," said Maurice, "listen, got others to see. Business hours, you know. There's a bag under the table, Justine, with a package in it. Whatever you do, don't leave without it."

"Is that what we're doing?" I said. "Transporting?"

Maurice looked at me, and I could feel Justine looking as well.

"Get to Galini," Maurice said. "You have enough folding?"

Justine said, "We're fine."

"Fuck, Justine." He took a leather currency file from his jacket, pulled a thick stack of bills from it, and laid them on the table. "Various shit," he said. "Liras, drachmas, and some other stuff mixed in. Six or seven hundred quid worth. Against your end of it."

"I said we have enough."

"A train to Athens for three." He looked at Darcy. "Two or three. A ship to the island. Buses, taxis. You'll have to stay in Galini at least a couple days, so a room or two."

"We have enough," she said.

He scooped up the paper and stuffed it back in the file, which he dropped in the side pocket of his jacket. "You bloody well better," he said. "And you make fucking sure you have the package when you get there."

"That's it?" I said.

"Just get there. Then wait. It's not a big place. Someone'll find you."

FOR SOME TIME AFTER HE'D gone, Justine dragged on her cigarette while staring at the table. I sipped at my beer and watched Darcy watch Maurice making his way around the room, sitting at a table here and there or hanging at the bar.

"He was serious about this being business hours," Darcy said. "I don't suppose you can tell me what that was all about."

"To be perfectly truthful," Justine said, "I don't really know."

"What's in the pack?"

She shrugged.

"But you're taking it."

"Yes."

"Just like that. You could get sent away forever where you're going if it's anything like it sounds."

Justine lit a new cigarette, the last one, from the ember of the one she was finishing.

"For what?" Darcy asked. "How much are you getting?"

Now Justine's face changed. For the first time around the girl, she started to look pissed off. She opened her mouth to speak, but before she could, Darcy cut in.

"How much? A few thousand? For that kind of risk?"

Justine said, "What do you care?"

"I don't. Not at all. It just makes my stomach hurt to see such pathetic losers getting pushed around and used."

"Who—" Justine said, then looked at me as if to say she didn't know what to say. She was struck dumb.

"—do I think I am?" said Darcy. "I'm somebody at least—which is to say I'm not nobody, unlike some of the people at this table."

"Holy shit," Justine said. "Don't you have a train to catch, little girl? Back to your nanny and your little chums?"

"I'm not the one with little friends," she said.

"Are you referring to Maurice? Little? Hardly, dear. Not someone you want to mess about with."

"Really? Is he in the same league as you two big-timers? Or does he at least make enough to get by? I'll tell you, I'm impressed. Con artist central, here we are."

It was then, of course, that I began to see how badly we'd misjudged. I didn't know the full extent of it yet, but I felt it. It made me cold at first, chilly. My stomach knotted and unknotted. Not that there was anything really dangerous about it; it was just that we'd misread things so badly. It hadn't happened before.

Justine, on the other hand, couldn't stop the act. She put on a shocked expression and said, "What?"

Darcy sat back in her chair and laughed, and I had to suppress a smile lest Justine see it.

"What do you call it? Grifting? Scamming? How much of an idiot— Is anyone really as stupid as you've taken me to be?"

Now Justine just sat, saying nothing. Waiting for it. I didn't know if what I was feeling was excitement or illness.

"You think I went out to that toilet you call a hostel because I wanted a glass of bad wine? Because I was swept off my feet? I have to admit I didn't see the spike coming. That was good. That was surprising. Weirdly vicious, I have to say. Way over the top. Sick, even, but effective. I'll give you that. What was it?"

Justine flicked off an ash and said, "GHB."

"Nobody ever taught you how to pick a stupid pocketbook? You've got to knock someone out to steal their money? Jesus. What else did you do to me?"

Justine shook her head and said, "Nothing, dear. We made sure you were safe."

"Well, thank you. So was there a plan? Milk the rich bitch as long as she lets you? Let her buy your tickets and your meals and your hotel room until she gets tired of it and goes back where she belongs?"

I nodded without realizing I was doing it. Justine didn't move.

"You're kidding, really, right? *I* was kidding. That's even more pathetic than I thought. I mean I was waiting for something. Some idea. You know, you call Daddy Warbucks and tell him you're holding Annie, and if he doesn't cough up a hundred grand, you'll snuff her. Something. I mean, God, all this for a train ticket and a room? Who are you people?"

"All right," Justine said. "Shut up, okay?"

Darcy looked out the window again.

"Who are you?" Justine asked her then.

"I'm only who I said I was: a girl from Ohio who's on a tour of the great art and architecture of Europe. And bored of it and wanting some distraction."

"Well, I guess you got some."

"I guess I did. Can I ask you something? Why didn't you take that money he put down here?"

"Because I'd owe him even more than I do now. And I hate owing him anything."

"Then why don't you do something about it? For starters, get your hands on as much of his cash as you can."

"Who— What do you know about *any* of this?"

"More than you'd guess, *Madre*. I know he's as much of a chump as you are. He's just got you scared for some reason."

"Oh, stop, will you?"

"I could get money out of him tonight before we leave here—lots of it."

"Really?"

"Yes."

"Then do it."

Darcy pulled her hands from beneath the table and laid the leather file on it.

"Oh," Justine said, "fucking hell. Are you insane?"

"I might be," Darcy said. "But there's a lot of cash here,

and now it's mine. See how it works? I don't owe him anything because he doesn't know I took it."

"Christ. You are mad."

"Are you scared?"

"*You* should be." But I knew who was the frightened one. Justine had on a face I'd never seen. Darcy pulled the wallet back off the table. "Do you have any idea what he'll do to you?"

"Nothing if I give it back to him and tell him you stole it—minus, of course, what you took from me. But he'll understand that. It's your rear he'll take it out on, not mine."

Justine stuck a finger into the empty cigarette pack, fished around, and said, "Fuck, I need a smoke."

"On the other hand, we can clean the cash out and leave the wallet someplace where he won't suspect it was us."

"We?" Justine said.

"There's more in there than he was going to give you—maybe a couple of thousand dollars' worth."

"What game are you playing?"

"Game?" said Darcy. "You mean what do I do besides travel around looking at ancient *merde*." Darcy pulled her big purse onto her lap, dug into it, and removed another pack of cigarettes, Marlboro Reds.

"Where do you get all these?" said Justine.

"Around," she said. Then she took out something else and laid it on the table. It was a wristwatch, a Clerc just like the one I'd stolen from the German and then lost.

I said, "Shit."

"Is it the same one?" asked Justine.

I picked it up, inspected it, slipped it on my wrist, and said, "Yeah." Then I took it off and set it down.

Darcy reached into her bag again and placed a small Bible covered in red leather beside the watch. It was Justine's. I'd seen her reading from it now and then but had never asked her about it.

"You complete and utter cunt," Justine said. "What could you possibly want with that?"

"Nothing," Darcy said. "I don't want any of this *caca.*" She then produced, in succession, a gold and silver monogrammed money clip, an ivory hair comb, a silver class ring set with a huge faceted blue stone, two more packs of cigarettes, three Zippo lighters, a journal embossed in gold with the word *Private,* a Mont Blanc fountain pen, a silver egg cup, half a dozen sterling dinner utensils, a magnifying glass, a plane ticket, a transistor radio, and, most improbably, an onyx-handled stainless steel folding knife, the blade of which must have been at least four inches long.

She said, "I have a problem. This . . . disease."

"Disease?" I said.

"I can't help it. I've been doing it since I was like ten. Shoplifting, picking pockets, even the occasional burglary, believe it or not. Usually those were just neighbors' houses. For a while all I stole was lingerie. I've been to *merde*loads of the best shrinks in Cleveland, Columbus, Pittsburgh, and even New York, therapists, twelve-step groups. No one could ever get me to stop. I even went to jail once. Then they put me in a mental ward for a while, but I was no crazier than anyone who worked there, and they knew it. When their stethoscopes kept disappearing, they kicked me out."

"Oh, for Christ's sake," Justine said and rubbed her eyes. Then she pointed at the smokes and said, "May I?"

"They're yours," Darcy said. "The lighters, too." Then, to Will, "Sorry about the watch."

"It's fine," I told her. "Can I have it back?"

"Well, it's yours, isn't it?"

"Not really."

"It is now. My gift to you."

"Thank you."

We then sat, the three of us, each stunned by this sudden sharing, this revelation, this laying of cards on the table.

"Well," Justine said at last, "I suppose if we're hanging it all out, we might as well finish. What are your plans?"

Darcy shrugged.

"You really want to go back to your tour?"

"No."

"You knew what was going on all along, didn't you?"

"Well, no. I mean not really."

"I mean when we offered you an escort."

"I had my hopes, you know? That we could hang out still. Delay things. I knew we were getting on the wrong train, if that's what you mean."

"And that pleased you."

"Yes."

"Then why don't you come with us?"

I felt another shock as her words settled.

They were silent until Darcy said, "Seriously?"

"Yes, of course," said Justine. "Just promise you'll stop nicking our shit. Of course you can keep nicking other people's."

"Oh, sure."

"And, again, there's the money issue."

"I'll pay," she said. "I've just come into a whole bunch of cash, see."

"That's not what I meant. That's not your effing money."

Darcy started to laugh then. It was a strange high-pitched squeal, incongruous with the rest of her but infectious nevertheless. I laughed, too.

"Oh, stuff it," Justine said, "both of you. It's not yours. You can't take it from Maurice."

"I already did. Here." She put the empty leather file back on the table and said to me, "Take it to the men's room and leave it on the floor by the toilet. Someone'll find it. It's all there but the cash."

"You've still got your cards."

"Yes. I can get the train tickets and whatever else we need."

"How much cash can you withdraw on the gold?"

"I don't know. Maybe a thousand."

"That should do. Then once you've withdrawn, you have to get rid of them. Throw them away."

"Yes."

"What will happen? You'll inform the tour?"

"I suppose."

"You must. Otherwise, they'll call in the authorities. We absolutely can't have that."

"Okay."

"And your parents? I imagine they'll be concerned."

"I'll take care of it."

"See that you do."

"What's in the package?"

"I really don't know," Justine said. "I don't."

"You're taking a huge risk then. They have narc dogs that sniff—"

Justine replied, "I doubt Maurice would enlist our help to move a small parcel of powder from Italy to Crete. Not very cost effective, you know? And I suspect that that sort of thing generally comes in the other direction. Why would you take it there if you can sell it for at least as much here?"

Darcy thought for a moment, then nodded. "Today," she said, "when we were sitting in the sun, I realized that you guys were the only people who had any idea where I was. God, I *loved* that feeling. Do you ever think about how right at a certain moment no one else who knows you in the entire world knows exactly where you are?"

"No," Justine said.

But I did. I knew exactly what she meant. It struck me just that way when Justine and I first went off together, but I confess the wonder of it had worn off. In the years since, though, I have found it again now and then, at odd moments, but never that profoundly.

"You could just disappear if you wanted."

"You can always do that."

"Can you?"

"You can. You're about to, and so am I. I'm knackered. I'm going to bed." She waited then, apparently for us to say we were going to join her. But when Darcy asked me instead if there was any place else I knew of that was open, and I said I supposed so, Justine regarded us briefly and then got up and left.

"Or we can just walk," said Darcy. "Do you mind walking?"

"I like to walk."

"Then let's."

Six

THEY FOUND A PAY PHONE not far from the American Café. She got through to an American operator and made it collect. If things went perfectly, Mommy and Daddy would be out and Ellie, the housekeeper-cook, would answer and take a message. But it was her father who accepted the charges.

"Hi, Daddy," she said.

There was a pause and then in his usual voice, low and modulated and so throaty it sounded almost vicious—it was the exact yang to Mommy's yin—he said, "Where in Jesus' name are you?"

"Gosh," she said, "it's so good to hear your voice, too."

"Darcy, goddammit. Those people called here. They said you just up and took the hell off or something. They didn't know what the hell happened."

He was a concrete contractor, Daddy was. He'd made millions of dollars paving over the shit that was Cleveland, as he put it. He was one of the biggest cement layers in the State of Ohio, and, he was fond of saying, there was one goddamn shitload of cement in Ohio. My eloquent dad, she'd called him to her friends.

"Well, I guess that's right," she said. "I did just up and take the hell off."

"What're you doing?"

"Having fun, Dad. Believe it or not."

"Darcy—"

"Look, I didn't mean to. It was a mistake. I went out with some friends and I got sick—"

"Drunk, you mean. Stinking, I bet. You're good at that, like your mom."

"Great. But no, actually I didn't get stinking. I missed the train to Florence, so my friends were going to bring me up, and we got on the wrong train."

"So where are you now?"

"Venice."

"What?"

"It's another city in Italy."

"Yeah, Darcy. I know that."

"It's beautiful, actually. I love it here."

"So how far is it to wherever you're supposed to be?"

"I don't know."

"Hadn't you better look into it? Get a ticket and get your ass over there?"

"Well, it's almost midnight here, so I can't do anything now. But I don't know. I like it here so much."

Another long pause. She could hear him smoking now. He only smoked when he was really pissed off.

"Darcy, goddammit—this was so expensive, this bullshit tour. If you were just gonna go off and wander around with some other drunks, then I coulda just got you a plane ticket."

"And that's what I said I wanted, isn't it, Dad? Do you remember that conversation? I said just get me a ticket and maybe a Eurail pass. That's all I asked for. But Mommy had like three heart attacks, and you were all 'You can't do that. A girl all alone over there.' "

"So you pull something like this."

"Listen," she said. She was crying now, but she covered the phone when she sniffed so he wouldn't pick up on it. "I was still thinking about going back to the tour. But I've decided now I'm not going to."

"What're you gonna do?"

"I don't know, Daddy. I'll send you a postcard. How's that?"

She hung up.

LATER, WILL HELD HER. THEY'D found a lonely bridge somewhere in the fog and the night, as alone as they could be, and she wept, and he kept her close to him until she had it all out, and he never asked a question. He just understood. She knew he understood. Everything. When she had calmed down and dried up, she looked up at him, and they kissed for the first time since that night in Rome. But this time it went on and grew more heated until he was pressing her back against the abutment and moving against her, and neither of them wanted to stop, but they finally did.

"Do you think AmEx is open?"

"I don't know."

"We should get money while we still can. He may shut off the card."

"Would he do that?"

"Oh, yes."

"Maybe we can get the tickets, too."

"Good," she said. "Let's hurry. Then we can have another drink. Someplace that's very, *very* not American."

WHEN THEY WENT IN, THE room was so dark that Darcy had to orient herself, even to find the bed. They were drunk, and buzzed as well from walking in the Venetian night and from the making out they'd done on another dark bridge somewhere in it. They'd held on to each other for a long time and pressed themselves together again, and she told him she wished it was an empty room they were going back to.

She listened now to Will undressing and tried to see where Justine was lying. Then she noticed, in the corner of the room, a floating orange bead, an ember. Justine was in the chair by the window, smoking. The glow brightened when she drew on it and threw an orange cast over the bedspread and Will's boxer-clad body as he got beneath it.

"C'mon," he whispered. He hadn't noticed Justine. Where, Darcy wondered, did he think she was? But he was just drunk. He wasn't thinking about anything. Well, maybe one thing.

She thought to say something but didn't know what exactly. And she thought Justine might speak to them, but she did not. The room remained silent. Will snuggled in and pulled the covers up to his neck. The orange light rose again, then fell.

It made her suddenly angry, Justine sitting there like that, silently chastising them, watching them, judging them. Darcy knew she was judging them.

She undressed—all the way. She hoped Justine could see every inch of it. She took off her shoes, socks, jeans, and the long-sleeved T-shirt she'd been wearing, and then she undid her bra, dropped it, and slipped out of her panties. She stood in the chill dark air so that when the cigarette glowed, it would illuminate all of her. Look at this, old woman.

Then she went around and got in the bed. The cold new sheets felt wonderful against her bare skin. Will lay in the middle, where he had slept the night before, between the women, though now it was only the two of them. Darcy turned her back to him and moved into him as she had that morning, shifting and moving it against him. He had an immediate erection or, rather, a continuation of the one he'd been pressing against her and that he'd probably had in some state since that morning. Poor man.

She reached behind her, took his hand, and pulled it over so that it lay against her belly. She continued to move against him and felt him move against her. As silently as they could, they writhed. She shifted her legs so that they were slightly parted and reached back again, found his cock, and guided it into her. And they moved that way, quietly, subtly, but enough so that before too long she felt him begin to climax. And she felt herself going with him. She wanted terribly to feel him come inside her, his warmth, knowing that she had caused it and that Justine was sitting there, hearing if not seeing it all. Will moved his hand to her breast and gripped it. He pressed his mouth into her back, into her hair, and he came so hard, she could hear his teeth grinding, could feel his entire body spasm. She took his hand in both of hers and held it tightly until they had finished.

He lay back, touching her still, but relaxed.

It was then that Darcy heard, in the quiet of the darkness, a sound she had not thought it possible to hear. It came from the chair by the window in the corner of the room where the orange glow had now been extinguished. At first she thought she must be imagining it or that Justine had had too many cigarettes or that all the speed was making her nose run. But as Darcy listened, she knew that Justine was weeping. And the thought of it made her dizzy with the power she held, and a sense of excitement, of raw possibility, that she did not remember having felt for a long, long time, and she wanted to think about it some more, to contemplate it, to roll around in it. But then she slipped almost immediately into the deepest sleep she'd had in ages.

December 15, 1987

Locanda Apostoli
Venice, Italy

Dear Whoever Daddy Has Sent After Me:

Welcome to Venice! It's a beautiful place. You should really take a little time out from your hot pursuit and walk around a bit, watch the sunlight coming off the canals, taste the wine, ride in a gondola. We saw the Bridge of Sighs this morning, early, before we had to check out, and it made me cry. You should go. And the Paolo San Marco. And, for a hoot, the American Café.

But I know you won't. You're surely one of Daddy's hard-ons-for-hire, an ex-cop, a private investigator, who knows what. A bounty hunter maybe! Anyway, I hope you're having fun, but I'm sure you're not.

So, to business: If you're reading this, you've caught up to me this far. I stayed in this very hotel for two nights. You're here because you traced the credit card charges I made. Easy work. But don't get used to that.

You are, of course, at least a day late, maybe more, but you're smart and probably mean, and Daddy has undoubtedly rented you a private jet and pilot, so you'll think of something. In the meantime, here's a little hint:

Sit by the phone. Don't move! You might miss me.

Your new friend,
Darcy

The Balkans

Seven

I COULD NOT SHAKE THE ODD dual emotions of trepidation and fascination that had wracked me since the scene in the diner the night before. In the Santa Lucia Station, Sunday evening, Justine sat apart from us and seemed to have collapsed into herself. She hardly spoke and did not eat or accept my offer of a cup of tea. Darcy was left in charge of finding the right train this time. It was as if Justine had abnegated all her powers to this girl and had taken to regarding me only at arm's length, as she had when we were first together.

In the very beginning, it had taken me a couple of days to make the decision to leave with her, although she'd allowed for that possibility the first night. During that time she stayed in a faded hotel in downtown Roanoke alone—that is, without inviting me up. She hugged me at the front door a couple of times but did not allow me so much as a peck on the cheek. After we took off and were sharing rooms, I guess I thought a more complete relationship would just naturally happen. How could it not? But of all things, she behaved demurely. She changed only in the bathroom. She slept either fully clothed or in a flannel neck-to-ankle nightgown that looked as old as she was. And she wouldn't let us get drunk. After the first few days, I was coming to believe I'd taken on a den mother rather than a partner. I had no idea how to act toward her, how she wanted me to act, and whether things were to continue in this vein. Otherwise, she fascinated me. What she was teaching me was both thrilling and abhorrent, so it wasn't like I was bored or anything. But I was attracted to her. Smitten. Crazy.

So one night I got into her bed. I don't know what I expected: that she'd get angry, kick me out not only of the bed but of her life, or she'd melt at my hot nearness and we'd fall into each other. But she did nothing. She just moved over to make room for me and went to sleep. And that was how we woke up. I didn't bother the next night, but then the night after that, she got in with me. I tried to kiss her, and she just turned away without saying anything but letting me lie against her back.

A week or so passed like this, and then a strange thing happened one morning. We woke up together in the same bed, as chaste as we had been, and as I lay looking at the ceiling, she raised herself on one arm and looked at me. And from that angle, in that thin light, I saw myself. I saw my face in her face—as if there were something physical of me in her. And it scared me so badly that I recoiled.

"My God," she said. "I know I look a fright in the morning, but I didn't mean to offend you."

"No," I said. "You look good."

"Well, you're a gentleman. Somebody raised you right."

"You do," I said. "It's not that. It's . . . just weird."

"Well, that's lovely then. I'll take weird over hideous."

"Not you. Me. Us, I mean. It's like we're . . . alike."

She looked away and said, "What do you mean?"

"I don't mean, you know, emotionally or how we act. I mean how we look. *Who* we are. Like you're me. Or I'm you."

"You are what's weird."

"Well, that may be, but what's between us is weird, too. Isn't it?"

"What is between us?"

"I don't know," I said. "I was hoping you'd tell me."

It wasn't long after this that she began to reduce the restriction on our drinking too much. And one night we did shots of Cuervo with lime slices in a decent hotel bar in Kansas City, paid for on the expense account of a lonely dental supplies salesman from Tulsa whom she'd shamelessly led on. (I was her little brother in these scenarios.) After we'd separated the guy from a wad of his cash and ditched him, and had fallen into our room, she informed me that I was a bad, bad boy and that it was all her doing, and she felt sorry for that. Then she laughed. I grabbed her suddenly and kissed her on the mouth. She struggled to refuse me, but I had her in a good grip and just forced it, something I had never done to a woman before. When I let her go, she slapped me on the side of the head so hard that my ear rang into the next day. And that, you might think, would've been that.

But I could see in her face that something had changed. Or been released. She had always seemed a particularly animated creature to me, alive in the way most people could never be. But now it was as if someone had discovered she was electric and had plugged her in.

I leaned in to kiss her again, but she pulled away and said, "Take your clothes off."

I looked at her a moment and said, "Wow. That was quick. Maybe we could—"

She grabbed my hair and pulled my head back until I fell onto one of the beds, and said into my ringing ear, "I said take your fucking clothes off."

And that's when it really began between us.

Although the subject of her initial disinclination toward anything physical would come up in the weeks and months that followed, and I asked repeatedly, she never revealed the reasons behind it. Except to say that she was actually a very traditional lady and didn't just go around leaping into the sack with any boy she happened to meet on the road.

BEFORE WE WERE TO BOARD the train, Darcy and I left Justine with the packs to find the restrooms. I returned first. Justine was squatting on the floor beside her pack, which was next to the new red nylon one Darcy had bought that morning before ditching her set of Vuittons. When I sat down, she said, "You have to listen to me." She spoke quietly. "You can't know me."

"What?"

"On the train. Act like you don't know me."

"For how long?"

"Until I say otherwise." She unzipped one of the exterior compartments on her pack, removed the pill bottle I'd last seen on her bed in the hostel, and handed it to me.

"It's up to you whether to risk carrying it over. I cannot. It'll probably be fine, but if it's not, you're in deep shit. If you're not comfortable with that, throw it away."

"What's going on?"

"You stay with her. Do you understand?"

"No."

"At all costs you stay with that girl. Whatever happens."

"Justine—"

"From now on if you see me, you're blank. Like you've never seen me before. Her, too. She has to act that way. Both of you. You explain it to her. And don't lose each other. And keep the packs in sight of at least one of you at all times. This is not a safe train. That's not too complicated for you, is it?"

"No. But why?"

"Just listen to me. Please. I'll be around," she said. "You may see me, but you don't know me. You can't—until I say. It's very important."

Masses of people flowed around us, backpackers and business travelers and couples. I said, "All right."

"If you get a window seat, there'll be a space between the seat and the outside wall. It'll be tight, but you can jam that bottle down in it, so if you get searched, it's not on you. If someone finds it, you know nothing about it. It was already there."

"By the seat."

"Yes. Then just make sure you don't change seats."

"Justine, I'm sorry. I don't know what you think is going on or whatever. I know you're mad."

"That's not what we're talking about. That's for later. Right now you have to listen to what I'm telling you and follow it exactly. If this gets fucked up, we're done—and I don't just mean with each other."

She put a fingertip to her mouth, kissed it, and reached up and touched my lips. Then she lifted her pack, slid it on, and walked toward the platform where our train waited.

THEN THERE WAS NO PLACE, only movement. The train would not arrive in Athens until Tuesday, a forty-hour ride, and other than small, smelly toilets, it had nothing in the way of amenities. There were just people—people jammed into the traveling compartments and along the hallways and even in the vestibules between the cars. Darcy called it a third world refugee train, and I knew it was certainly the closest thing to one she'd ever experienced. But she laughed when she said it, and I could see the rush in her eyes. I wondered if she was aware of how much Justine would have hated that. I didn't have a clue anymore what Darcy was aware of. She was a cipher, that's all. But I could almost hear Justine hissing, "No one has a right to be thrilled by something this utterly shitty."

The compartment held eight seats, four facing four. I had one on the window, and Darcy sat beside me, her feet on the edge of the seat, pressed against the back of her thighs, her arms around her knees, chin resting on top of them. She watched. I don't think she moved from that position until we hit the last stop in Italy, at the edge of the Yugoslav border.

Then someone said, "*Regardez!*"

Darcy leaned toward me and said, "Watch out," and at that moment, as if her saying it had somehow announced that the siege was allowed to begin, the door to our compartment slammed open and people from the hallway pressed in—refugee people, as Darcy called them. One slid open the window, and Western goods began to fly into the compartment from the platform outside. It was as if some magical capitalist lateral storm had begun to blow: designer jeans, bottles of Champagne and Italian wines, plastic-encased toys from Mattel and

Hasbro, wallets, running shoes, dress shoes, women's leather boots, raincoats, winter coats, leather jackets, tins of cookies, tins of dried fruits, boxes of teas, packages of underwear. All of these flowed into the compartment and were flowing into all the compartments along the whole train. It was the big smuggle. Accomplices bought the stuff in the West and transported it to the East, bypassing the censors and taxmen and culture ministries. In this way the proletariat had its fun and the free market worked, and there was nothing to be done about it.

Darcy screamed, "My God! It's fabulous."

The goods piled around our ankles. She picked up a bottle of wine to examine it, but someone snarled and snatched it away.

"You better be careful," I said.

"This is so wild."

"Do they always do this?"

She shouted in French across to the man who had warned us. He said something and nodded.

And then it ended as it had begun—suddenly. The window snapped closed, the goods vanished as though they'd never existed, the compartment emptied of all but the eight of us seated there, and the train—as if its sole reason for pausing on the Italian side was to allow this taking on of merchandise, this polluting of the East—started again and crept forward to the border.

SOMETIME AFTER MIDNIGHT, WHEN WE had all finally managed to begin to sleep, the door to the compartment opened, and someone reached in and switched on the overhead light. I snapped awake, squinting, and started to say, "Hey!" Then I saw that it was a man in a snuff-brown wool uniform. He looked at me.

"American?" the man said. "Canada? Brit?"

I shielded my eyes against the light and tried to make out the man's face. He was a guard or an officer of some kind. The others were waking up now.

"American, Canada, Brit?" the man said.

Darcy raised her hand like a good schoolgirl and said, "American."

"Come."

"Me, too," I said, although I had considered saying nothing in hope that the man would leave. I felt what was coming in my stomach.

The man nodded and crooked his finger.

The others in the car watched us. No one else said anything. I looked back at our bags and then at the others in the car, silently imploring them to let no one touch them, Justine's admonition playing in my head. As we left, another guard reached inside and shut off the light.

We were directed toward the far vestibule where most of the other passengers who had gathered wore the official overheated-refugee-train American student travel outfit of T-shirt and Adidases or Nikes. The refugees who had jammed the hallways and vestibules were gone. We were filed off into the night, from which I could see other guards through the windows. We were pointed across an adjacent track toward a small lighted building, a kind of shed or garage.

"What is it?" Darcy asked.

"I don't know."

We were fairly far north and somewhat above sea level. My breath, the breath of all of us, curdled into dense clouds.

"They should have told us to get coats or something," Darcy said.

"I doubt they know any English," said a woman waiting behind us, "besides 'American, Canada, Brit.' "

"Do you know what this is about?"

The woman shook her head.

"Pass-a-port," one of the guards shouted. "Pass-a-port!"

"So I was wrong," the woman said.

The guards were circulating now, yelling out, "Pass-a-port!" and collecting them.

"They can't do that," the woman said. "They're not allowed to confiscate an American passport. It's like in the Geneva convention or something."

"Well," I said, "are you going to tell them no?"

"Judas priest," the woman said.

One of the guards took our passports and left us there in the dark and the cold. Up ahead we could see that the first group was inside the shed now, standing at some sort of counter.

"This is really crazy," the woman said.

"It's like here we are," Darcy said, "behind the Iron Curtain. No passport, no coat, no luggage, no nothing in the middle of the night. If they wanted to totally screw us, they could do it."

"That's right," the woman said. "Who's to stop them?"

"It's not exactly the Iron Curtain. It's Yugoslavia."

"Close enough," the woman said.

"Wow," Darcy said. "Look at the moon."

It was full and huge, and it illuminated us. It was the only light, in fact, in the emptiness between the train and the guard's shed.

"At least there's that," I said. "The same old moon."

Darcy and I pressed together. She hugged my arm to her chest, and as we crept forward, I felt her trembling. Then a shout came from inside the shed. One of the guards was yelling something in whatever language they spoke there. Another one shouted something back, and then one of them came out. He was leading a passenger by the arm. It took a beat for me to realize that it was Justine.

Darcy looked at me but did not say anything. I had told her what Justine said, and Darcy seemed to accept it without question, as if it were a normal thing to have happen on a night train heading into Yugoslavia.

The guard walked Justine back along the line of shivering Americans, Canadians, and Brits. Two other guards, looking very important, followed. It was a procession, a parade, perhaps meant as a demonstration: This is what you get in the late General Tito's Yugoslavia if you do not behave.

In the moonlight I could see her face plainly as they led her past, but it revealed nothing, and she did not so much as glance at me. They led her to the train, which the three of them boarded with her.

"Oh, shit," I said to myself, though apparently not silently because Darcy said, "Stop it." Then she said, "You know what to do."

She sounded like Justine at that moment, and I looked at her, half expecting her to be Justine, half not believing that I was here with this woman, a different woman, a woman I had just met, and that Justine, with whom I had lived and slept and cried and made love for two years, was being interrogated by storm troopers, and maybe she would be gone then. Maybe this was how it happened, the big things, the huge shifts and changes—just like that. You got on a train, and when you got off a couple days later, your life was different.

After a few minutes, Justine and the three guards emerged from the train, one of the guards carrying her pack. They led her back past the line and into the shed.

Darcy would not meet my eyes. She was refusing me even the exchange of a knowing glance. She was cold inside, I thought, as cold as Justine could be. Maybe that was a truth about all women, that they could be as hard and chilly as they needed. I hadn't known too many women, and none nearly as well as I knew Justine, but that was the impression I'd gotten.

I looked back toward the train and let myself sink into the coldness until it became warmth. Darcy had moved in front of me, with her back against me, so I could smell her hair and her skin, and was able to lose myself in that. Soon we were at the shed door. It was simply a makeshift processing center where they matched your passport to your face and mangled your name, and you nodded and agreed with them. They stamped a forty-eight-hour transport visa in your passport that allowed you to travel through the country but not to get off the train.

When we got up to the counter, we could see into a back room where Justine's pack had been gutted and its contents laid out all over the floor. The three guards who had taken her into custody had been joined by two others, one a woman, the other in a darker uniform that I guessed marked him as a superior of some kind. Justine sat on a straight chair, hands pressed between her knees, staring at nothing. Her sweater had been removed, and her blouse was unbuttoned to her belly and opened so that her breasts were visible. She made no effort to hide them. The man who had led her away was talking excitedly to the others, and they back to him, all of it sounding like yelling.

"Do you understand anything?" I asked Darcy.

She shook her head.

Now the superior officer was holding up a flashlight with one hand and pointing with the other toward something farther back in the shed. He was speaking to the female guard, and she in turn said something to Justine and motioned for her to get up. Now Justine looked up at me. She held the gaze, and I held it, too, so that we had a moment together. I wanted to cry out to them to leave her alone, to not take her into the back room with the flashlight, please not to, she had done nothing, she carried nothing. Then she rose to her feet and went back with the woman guard.

She had known, I realized. She had anticipated everything.

"Okay," said the guard behind the counter and handed me my passport. "You go."

We were back in the warm darkened compartment, Darcy holding tightly on to me and resting her head against my arm, for over an hour before the train finally began to move again. I was certain the delay was because of Justine. I wondered if she was on board. Only after we began to move and I felt down alongside the seat for the plastic bottle of pills, which was still there, did I doze.

Sometime before dawn, while Darcy was sleeping, I extricated myself from her grasp and found the small penlight I kept in an outside pocket of my pack. I opened the pack, shined the light in, and moved things around. I found nothing missing and nothing other than what I'd packed. Then I opened Darcy's pack, which was next to mine on the steel rack. It had two large zippered pockets on the face of it and several long ones along the side, but I opened the main compartment. Tucked into an inside pocket and secured beneath a couple pairs of socks I found a narrow package, a box wrapped neatly in plain brown paper and heavily sealed with clear packing tape so that there was no possibility of opening it enough to have a peek inside. It was the package Maurice had delivered to us at the restaurant. I had seen it the previous morning when Justine was repacking. I asked her what it was or what she thought it was, but she'd merely shrugged.

Now, whatever it was, Darcy was the one transporting it. As always, Justine had known exactly what she was doing. She'd continued to use this girl, who was now an unwitting, unknowing mule in the service of Maurice's operation.

IN THE RUSH OF LEAVING and in the face of Darcy's coming with us, of her altering her life and ours, I had not thought enough about laying in supplies. Plus I had assumed, although Justine had intimated otherwise, that we could get something on the train. But there was nothing to be had, and those who had thought ahead tended to hoard. The two bottles of wine and the bread that Darcy and I had brought were gone by the end of the first night, and the effect of the wine was to make us thirstier than we would have been otherwise. So by Monday afternoon, as we passed into the heart of what was still a discrete political entity, we had stopped remarking on the primitive countryside or the bits of our respective pasts that we'd started to whisper to each other or the unexpected pleasure we felt in simply being there together, because we had begun to die of thirst. We were not on the verge of death—probably we'd have made it to Athens with no lasting ill effects—but we were dehydrated enough that it changed the way we acted, altered how we felt, and began to frighten us. I had even decided, although I had not grown quite desperate enough to act on it, to find Justine if she was still on the train and break my vow to ignore her and ask her how to solve the problem of water—because surely she would know.

But before that happened, we arrived at the station in Belgrade. We were dozing on each other, a light sticky uncomfortable sleep, the sleep of escape and boredom and desperation, when the slowing of the train awakened me. I looked out from my slumped-down vantage and saw the overhead wires of a city and then the scaffolding over the platform of the depot. I was not roused to sit up and look outside until one of the other passengers stood, lowered the central window of the compartment, and leaned out. People in the hallway were hanging out the windows, too, and there seemed to be some excitement about it. I sat up further. Lines of people, local Belgradians become temporary vendors, had massed along the platform and were holding up wrapped sandwiches and cans of Coca-Cola. The other passenger, an Italian man, was waving a thousand-lira note and shouting something that sounded fairly desperate.

"Darcy," I said, nudging her awake. "Hurry up."

"Hmm," she said.

"Dollars."

"What?"

"Do you have some dollars? Anything?"

"Why?"

"Coke."

This brought her up. She did not even look to see what I was talking about but stood on her seat and dug into her purse, which was on top of her pack on the shelf above us. She handed me a five.

"No ones?"

"Just take it."

I leaned out with the note pinched between my fingers, and a boy was there immediately.

"Coke," I said.

The boy held up a single can.

"No," I said. "More." I held up five fingers.

The boy said something and looked around. There wasn't time to barter here.

"Three," I said.

"No," the boy said and held up two. I gave him the five.

We got sandwiches, which Darcy was loath to trust but hungry enough to risk.

"Does anyone have water?" she said.

"I don't know."

"Let me try." She leaned out the window and called out "water" in four different languages, but none of the sellers reacted. "Coke!" she said, and several came running then. She managed to buy four more cans (at a much better rate than I'd managed) just as the train began to move.

And so we were saved by Western goods and currency. The following morning we awoke, stinky and miserable and foul-mouthed, to Greece gliding past our windows.

"I'd pay a thousand dollars for a shower right now," Darcy said.

"All right. You give me a thousand dollars, and I'll see that you get a shower as soon as we hit Athens."

She laughed.

"Are you having fun?" I asked her.

"I'm not sure if that's exactly what you'd call it, but it's something."

"You're happy."

"Mmm. I am now."

"Amazing what a few cans of Coke'll do for you."

"That and you."

"You'd rank me up there with a can of Coke?"

"Higher, even. A little. Are you amazed?"

"No one's ever said anything so nice about me."

"Oh, I know lots of nice things to say about you."

"Really?"

"Shall I say them?"

"Yes, please."

"Not now."

"When?"

"Mmm, we'll find a time—and a place."

"I'd kiss you—"

"I'd let you—"

There had been no way for us to brush our teeth during these forty hours.

"Soon."

"Soon," she said.

Eight

Justine found them sitting on a wooden bench near the front doors of the Athens station, looking displaced and tired. Exhausted. As if they'd been made to walk all the way from Venice. She couldn't figure it. She'd dozed most of the way after the little pseudo-Commie-fuck shakedown—a desperate bit of post-Tito machismo, even by the woman, that you knew was a kind of last hurrah because that slum country was coming apart at the seams, or was going to soon enough, and everyone knew it, even the pathetic border guards. That she'd been sitting upright the whole way and that she'd had nothing to eat or drink mattered not at all. She could think of nothing she'd rather have done than just sit somewhere, alone, unknown, unspoken to, and looked to by no one for sustenance or courage or sex or ideas or even a goddamn smile. That and sleeping. It was all she was planning to do on the ship to Crete as well and once they got there. To sleep—it was her highest, most gnawing aspiration.

"You two jessies look scared shitless," she said to them. "Are you nervous or what?"

"Do we know you?" Darcy said.

"What do you mean?"

"Are we allowed to talk to her highness now?" The girl delivered this in her most exaggerated Little Bitch tone. "To be seen with you? To acknowledge that we know you?"

"You did understand what that was all about, didn't you?" Justine sat down beside them. "I mean, you did happen to notice what went on?"

"Oh, absolutely."

"Then why are you taking the piss now?"

"That's just me, I guess," Darcy said. "Always making fun. But what else can I do? I'm just the stupid little girl along for the ride who you can use for whatever you need. Some cash? Some heavy lifting? A sucker for a little cross-border transportation? I'm your girl."

"You'd better shut up, sweet, or you'll fuck us all up."

"Oh, you don't know the half of it."

"So you couldn't help it?" Justine said to Will. "Couldn't manage to keep a secret from your new squeeze? Are you in love already, ickle boy?"

"He didn't say a word about anything," Darcy said. "Not one. It's just the same old boring thing—me not being quite as stupid as you make me out to be."

"Yes, yes, well, I can take it off your hands now if you find it so upsetting."

"The only thing that upsets me is that you didn't ask. Didn't bother to explain anything. You just set me up to take your fall."

"My fall?"

"If that's how you want it, then fine. Consider me set up."

"I was trying to keep us all from copping it, you stupid little cow."

"And we didn't," Darcy said, "so you're a genius. But keep this in mind: You're also without your precious little package."

Justine looked at her and then at Will. "What does that mean?"

Darcy shrugged.

"Will?"

"I have no idea, Justine. You didn't bother to tell me anything, either. She didn't tell me anything. So how am I supposed to know anything? I don't."

"Well, that's true. Christ forbid you should have to climb out of the bliss of your ignorance for a moment. Can we just get on with it? I'm very bored right now."

"And I'm tired," Darcy said. "Can we sleep?"

"Not yet," said Justine. "We need to be on the ship that leaves today."

"Tonight," said Darcy. "I picked up a *Let's Go* in Venice, and I've had a lot of time to read it. I found a place where you can pay for just half a day—the Merry Trumpet Guesthouse."

Justine said, "It's not some posh hotel, just dorm rooms and cots, like a hostel."

"So you know it."

"Course."

"Well, I don't care at this point. And I assume I'm still paying, so I don't really want a hotel. The credit cards are finished now. Whatever we have, that's all there is."

"It's never all there is."

"You're right," said Darcy. "But I just want a nap, so can we go there?"

"You do still have it, don't you? The package?" said Justine.

"Probably," Darcy said.

JUSTINE REMEMBERED A LITTLE GYRO stand in the alley behind the guesthouse and took them there after they'd dropped off their bags. They stood against a wall, eating like refugees and drinking Pepsis.

"God," said Will, "it's the best food I've ever had."

"The best?" Little Bitch said in her finest faux petulance.

"Second best. Rome was the best."

Now the girl smiled.

"It's so cute," said Justine. "The two of you already collecting memories."

"Justine," said Will, "can we stop now?"

"I assumed we had stopped," she said. "I thought that's what this was all about."

"I didn't mean that."

"Really?"

"Listen," said Darcy, "I'm beat. You two can work this out. I'm going to lie down." She left them, but Justine could tell that Will didn't want her to go.

FOR A TIME THEY WALKED without speaking. The day was glorious, and when they passed along certain roads where the city opened up, they could see the Acropolis. When that happened, Justine felt the way she had felt that day in Venice—as if she were inhabiting a postcard. There were no clouds or even hints of clouds in the sky, and the color of it was so concentrated, so simultaneously sharp and deep that after a while it hurt to look at it. It was not usually like that here with the city's chronic polluted haze. Before, the sky had always looked diluted, washed out, but today it could be a sky from Montana or Iowa or that place in Virginia where she had finally found Will. It was certainly not a sky you ever saw in England.

"So," she said.

"So what happened on the train?"

"I managed to get my name on a list a number of years ago. It was a stupid thing that shouldn't have happened, but it did. I got out of any real trouble, but I was on the list. Apparently I still am."

"How bad was it?"

"It wasn't pleasant."

"Right."

"So," she said again.

"I don't know," Will answered. "I don't know what's going on."

"With regard to what?"

"Anything. Any fucking thing."

"Poor Will."

"Don't make fun of me."

"I'm not, baby boy. I'm really not. I feel bad."

"Why?"

"For you. About all of this."

"All—"

"This shit. We have to do this, and I'm sorry about that. I wish I hadn't had to drag you into it."

"Did you? Have to, I mean."

"I don't know. Maybe not. You can leave."

"When?"

"Anytime you want. Right now."

"I don't want to leave."

WHEN SHE FINALLY FOUND HIM, she'd been looking for a year. The family who had taken him from England many years before had done a real job covering everything. They had changed his name and had even gone so far as to get him a U.S. birth certificate with a new name, which she wasn't sure was even legal. She'd had nothing to go on except the name of the man in London who had arranged everything. And it hadn't been strictly legal either, of course, which had made finding him after all that time tricky. When she knocked on the door of a scrubby flat in Roxbury, he answered. She said who she was, and he just looked at her as if she were a dream he'd forgotten to wake up from.

"How ever did you find me?" he said.

"With some difficulty," she told him.

"I can imagine."

"But I had a bit of a head start. I'm Maurice's ex-wife. Did you know we'd got married?"

"I had no idea." It was through Maurice, in fact, this business they were in, that she had met this man during the marketing of the infant Will.

"I want to find him," she said.

"Why?"

"I don't know. I need to."

He shook his head and then asked her in. After he brewed a pot and poured for them both in large stained crockery mugs, he said, "Leave him alone. Why upset things now? He was a baby. I doubt he knows he had a life before the one he has now."

"I'm sure he doesn't."

"So why?"

"I said I don't know. Maybe I won't bother him. Maybe I just need to see him, see that he's okay. Maybe I'll just look and leave."

"I'm sure he's fine. They were a good family. Solid. Well enough off."

"What did he do? The father."

He looked at her for a long and uncomfortable moment, as if he were deciding something, then finally said, "It was some kind of foreign service."

"He was a diplomat?"

"I don't know, really. He was with the American government, and he could afford our fees, yours and mine and Maurice's. I kept no records, you know."

"Nothing?"

"It was safer that way for everyone."

"Except maybe the boy."

"Do you really think that's true? You didn't then."

"No," she said. "I still don't." She began to cry then and didn't know why. She had no stake in this, not really. He'd be an utter stranger to her if she were ever to track him down. Perhaps it was just out of frustration at running into a wall after months of on-and-off looking for this man. Perhaps underneath it all she still felt something for the boy. Perhaps that was what this was about, although she didn't know how it could be.

"I could pay you," she said. The flat was as shabby inside as the neighborhood was outside. What he had been two decades earlier, whatever sort of hustler deal maker, he wasn't anymore. She imagined he had done some prison time, though she had no way of knowing that.

"How much?"

"How much would you need? And what would it buy me?"

He crossed his legs and looked out his window into the cracked but quiet street. "I remember a last name," he said.

"That's all?"

"And that he, the father, had a certain mark, an extreme mark."

"No first name?"

"I'm afraid not, though I remember his wife's, oddly enough. She was so happy, she wept all the way from Winchester back to London."

"How much?"

"I don't care."

She had two hundred quid with her, which she laid on the low table in the center of the room.

"Dolores," he said.

"Are you kidding?"

"Not at all. And the husband was Mr. Symons, with a *y* and one *m*."

"Right."

"His hands were all scarred. He'd been burned." He rubbed his own together when he said this. "You almost never saw it. He wore gloves most of the time, but on the day we picked up the boy, he didn't for some reason."

"My God," she said. "I'd forgotten that. The scarring."

"Yes. It looked rather like plastic, didn't it?"

JUSTINE AND WILL WALKED FOR nearly an hour, saying little until they finally approached the guesthouse once more. Justine felt nicely exhausted. It was a good idea that Little Bitch had had, to find a place to nap before their departure. She really was a smart girl.

"What do you want, Will?" she asked when they turned back onto the street of the Merry Trumpet.

"Just not to have to worry so much."

"Then don't."

"That's easy to say, but starvation makes it kind of hard to do."

"You haven't starved. Don't be dramatic."

"I've been hungry. Weak from being hungry. Dizzy. It was never like that before. We had fun and plenty of whatever we needed. But something happened. You changed."

"I know."

He sat on a bench and looked across at the guesthouse. He said, "And that's all right. But if I need to start making my own way, I have to know."

"What about us?"

"What about us? I don't know what you want. That little thing at the hostel was the first time in like two months."

"Little thing," she said. "That's what it was?"

"No. I liked it."

"I did, too. But you're shagging the little bitch now, aren't you?"

"Don't, please."

"Well, aren't you?"

"Where would we have? We've been on a stinking train for two days, and you can't do much there."

"I wouldn't put it past you two."

"Look, I don't know what I'm doing—with her, with you, with whatever."

"Who do you want?"

"It's not that simple."

"Of course it is."

"If you're not going to do anything, if you're just going to be a meth-crazed depressive, then I don't know if I want to be around you."

"But you still love me?"

"Yes."

"Are you shagging her?"

"No, Justine. For Christ's sake."

"Well, that night in Venice you sounded awfully fucking friendly."

"I didn't know you were there. I was pretty plastered."

"All right," she said. "Don't get excited." She sat beside him and put her hand on his arm, and when he didn't pull away, she took that as a promising sign.

HE HAD NEVER GLOMMED ON to the fact that their connection predated his meeting her in Virginia, though she knew that at times he had glimpsed the deeper linkage, recognized it—their physical similarity—but had no form to put it into, and so was unable to name it. There had been from the first a palpable vibe between them, and it had made things awkward as well as easy in the beginning, especially regarding their physical relationship. She'd never told him the story, in any case. She just showed up in his life one day, a happenstance meeting of strangers at a bar he frequented. He had no idea she'd been watching him for weeks, that she had managed with nothing more than his father's last name, the fact of his government service, and the help of a very expensive private investigative service out of Arlington to track him to this small, pretty town on the suburban edge of northern Roanoke. He knew only that she was a woman who bought him a drink and with whom he'd felt an instant bond—and that he was looking for something the likes of which he hadn't figured out until she offered him the chance to go on the road with her to see some of his country and who knew what else.

Now, across from the Merry Trumpet in Athens, he stood up. What a lad he was, so strong and so tall.

"All right," he said.

"Yes? Is it?"

He nodded. "Now can we sleep?"

"Do you still have that little bottle of candy I gave you?"

"She's got it."

"What the hell for?"

"I told her about it on the train. I was just going to leave it there. I didn't want to worry about having it on me anymore. But she said she'd carry it." He paused. "You don't need one anyway. You should sleep while you can."

"I slept on the bloody train for two days, didn't I? I didn't take anything, so I think I deserve one now."

"You deserve one?"

"Why would you give them to her? What is it with you two? It doesn't even make sense."

"I told you: She's carrying the package, and she said she might as well carry that, too. I think it turns her on or something. The risk."

"She's so whacked, that girl. And you, you go right along. You do everything she says. She's got you right by the curlies, doesn't she?"

He closed his eyes, exhaled loudly through his nose, and looked all put upon. He said, "I'm going to sleep."

"I'm going to have a smoke."

"We should probably be out of here by, what, six?"

"A little after. We'll meet you in the lobby then."

He walked across the street and into the building.

As Justine finished her cigarette, she watched the traffic. She felt more tired now than ever, and the cars looked nice moving the way they did. She was close enough to the curb that she could feel the breeze they generated, and for some reason that made her feel more tired than she had. He was right. She did need to sleep. She had lied. She had catnapped in that half-awake and unsatisfying manner that was worse than not sleeping at all, that you woke up exhausted from. More sweat than dreams.

When she looked across at the guesthouse, she was surprised to see Will still standing in the lobby, just inside the open doorway. He was talking to two men. They wore sport coats and dress shirts with open collars. As she watched, she gathered that they were keeping him there, pressed against the front desk. Then Will did a strange thing. He looked at her. It seemed deliberate, that he meant for her to see it. It was too far to make out his expression, and of course the traffic precluded her hearing anything. One of the men followed his gaze and looked at her, too.

And then Justine looked up. Perhaps some movement had caught her eye. There, in a small round window on the second floor landing where she and the girl had walked up to the women's dorm to drop their bags, Justine saw her face. The girl's. Darcy's. Looking out. Looking at her. She was watching Justine. She was waiting for something. You could see that about her. Otherwise she'd be sleeping.

Justine looked at Will and the two men again. She stood up. As she did, Will reached into his jacket pocket, pulled out a red bandana, and wiped his face. It was not a gesture he ever made. He carried it for the same reason she carried a red scarf that she never wore. It was a sign, a warning. They had worked this out early in their partnership after an incident in a bar in Denver where Justine was working the place for donations to the Red Cross collection box they had nicked from outside the chapel in Denver Memorial Hospital. She was doing well, too, having a good day. They had cleared maybe $50 when Will, who was sitting at the end of the bar, saw a man coming down a back staircase and knew it was trouble. He tried to signal her, tried with his hands to warn her without being obvious, but she hardly glanced at him. And so the man, the owner, got her by the collar and dragged her, choking, to the rear door and pushed her out into the snow. Will eased himself out the front door and went around and found her there, swearing and trying to pick up the change that had scattered when the box broke.

Red for danger. It was a simple thing. If you flash it, it means get out. Go.

But she had a hard time accepting that this was that. That here of all places, in Athens, with a package that meant a fortune to them in the end if they delivered it or an abyss of grief if they didn't, Will should show red.

She looked up at the girl again. It was her. She'd done something. Justine could smell it.

The men were coming outside now, pulling Will along with them. Pointing at her. Waving up the street. A waiting car began to move.

She looked at Will one last time and then did what she had to, what she had no choice but to do.

Justine ran.

Nine

After she planted the bottle of pills in Justine's bag and told the clerk at the Merry Trumpet that this woman had been trying to sell her drugs, and after the clerk called the police and they interviewed her and buttonholed Will and questioned him, and after Justine had somehow figured it out and took off, Darcy checked them out and led Will to a small café across the street and a little ways down the block from the Merry Trumpet. She bought them a pot of tea and some pastries, and then left him to find a pay phone. Armed with an entire roll of ten-drachma coins, she reached an operator who understood enough English and Italian to put her through to Venice and the Locanda Apostoli. Darcy loved languages and absorbed them. She was fluent in French, passable in Italian and Spanish, and could order a meal in German, Dutch, Japanese, and Mandarin. Aside from numerous childhood trips to the Continent and Asia, mostly with her mother (her father couldn't stand those "faggot Frenchies and the like" or the "oily zipperheads"), she'd gone, on and off, to a very good, very exclusive boarding school in Pennsylvania and also belonged to the Alliance Française and the Istituto Italiano of Greater Cleveland. So when the clerk she reached at the Locanda spoke very little English, she managed to communicate her name and the fact that it was she who had left the note when she checked out. She asked whether anyone had shown up asking about her.

"Ah," the young female clerk said. *"Sì. Sì. Era qui."* He was here.

"*Non è ora là?*" Darcy asked.

"*No.*"

He'd checked in but only stayed a few hours, the girl said, after they gave him Darcy's letter. But he had left a forwarding number—in Athens, Greece.

Darcy felt a slight chill when the girl said that, a chill of shock that the man had not only gotten on to her this quickly but that he was already so close—in the same city, maybe only blocks away.

But it was a chill of thrill, too, that this was a real chase, that this man knew exactly what he was doing and, apparently, what she was doing, too.

She dialed the local number and spoke in English with the clerk. A moment later the room phone was ringing, and a moment after that a man said, "Hello."

"Did you like my note?"

"Darcy?"

"Yes."

"Well," he said, "I did like it. Thank you. I liked it very much."

"Seriously?"

"I am. And I took your advice. Before I left, I went and saw that bridge."

"And did you cry?"

"I'll never admit it."

She liked his voice, and this fact surprised her, too. She had expected some gruff midwesterner, some hard guy in the same league as her father, but this man didn't sound like that at all. He sounded smart—or, rather, educated. Erudite. Like someone who, say, taught English Renaissance Lit. He had an accent, not Ohio but a sort of East Coast drawl or slant that almost had a certain English shading to it. He bent his *a*'s and spoke without quite opening his mouth.

"I have to tell you," she said, "that I'm impressed."

"That I saw the bridge?"

"Well, yes. But that you're already in Athens, too. That's a pretty neat trick."

"Not really. You put the train tickets on AmEx."

"Ah," she said. She'd anticipated that he'd get here, just not this quickly.

She said, "What's your name?"

"Matthew."

"Matthew what?"

"Raines."

"You're not what I expected."

"No?"

"You're not a cop, are you?"

"Much worse than that. I'm a lawyer."

"Are you kidding?"

"No."

"What's a lawyer doing chasing after a spoiled runaway?"

"Well, getting paid for it, of course."

"Of course. Is this what you do?"

"Mmm, I do all kinds of things. A funny thing happened after law school. I realized that practicing law bored the life out of me."

She laughed.

"Contracts. Trials. I wanted to be out doing something."

"So you chase people."

"Well, not all the time. You'd be amazed at the weird circumstances that can benefit from the subtle touch of a legal hand."

"Hmm. And I'm a weird circumstance?"

"Well, I had done some work for your father before, and so he called me about this. It's not your usual missing person sort of thing. You're not really missing, for one thing. And this is Europe, so there are all kinds of issues that could come up, you know, diplomatic, criminal, psychological, physical."

"You sound very smart. Where did you go to law school?"

"Ohio State."

"Very good. Undergrad?"

"Duke."

"Wow. Impressive. Are you from the South?"

"Well, south Jersey."

"You and Bruce."

"I grew up just outside Philly, the great suburbs. So what are we doing, Darcy Arlen? Can you tell me?"

"Absolutely," she said. "We're having a trip."

"Mmm, yes. And are we enjoying it?"

"Very much."

"Good. But your father's really worried. You know that."

"No, I don't. Daddy's really something, but I'm not sure worried is it. Pissed off. Embarrassed. Humiliated."

"He's worried, Darcy. Believe me. I saw him. It's a nasty world out there."

"And a beautiful one."

"To be sure. Why don't you let me catch up to you just to keep an eye? I won't interfere, and I won't tattle."

"That would defeat the whole point, wouldn't it?"

"What is the point?"

"Exactly," she said. "I like you, Matthew the lawyer. So here's a clue: Do you play the trumpet?"

"What?"

She laughed. "Be merry, Matthew. See you soon. Maybe." She hung up.

AFTERWARD, SHE DUCKED INTO A tourist shop, bought an overpriced pair of cheap binoculars, and then rejoined poor Will, who seemed numb. She was curious as to how long it would take Matthew to find the Merry Trumpet. Her obvious hint was probably enough, but then she realized that all the police activity would leave a hot trail. It was very possible he'd find a way onto that as well.

And sure enough, it wasn't twenty minutes later that she saw a cab pull up at the Merry Trumpet and a largish Americanish-looking man get out and go in. He was inside about fifteen minutes, and when he came out, he stood for several seconds on the sidewalk, looking around—enough time for her to get the glasses on him.

He certainly stood out in that city. Pale pinkish, blond, khaki-suited, bespectacled. Blue-eyed, undoubtedly. It wouldn't be hard to see him coming. He wasn't particularly handsome. He was a bit doughy, but he looked as smart as he sounded.

She had just decided she liked his face when he ducked his head and got into the waiting car.

Well, she thought. One day the two of them would sit down over drinks—something southern; juleps, maybe, or special minty vodka martinis—and have a good talk and a laugh about all this. But for now she needed to leave him behind again. She was paying cash, so he wouldn't have such an easy time of it, but she'd help him along when the time came.

She watched until he got back into the cab and left. Then she told Will it was time for them to go.

THE MEDITERRANEAN. IN ALL HER travels she'd never so much as glimpsed it. And now she was riding on it, crossing it to the oldest Western civilization of them all, far older than Rome, much older than Greece, the true cradle of the West: Iraklion, Crete, port of the ancient city of Knossos. The highest flowerings of the culture she'd come here to study, the most glorious achievements of Western man, the Raphaels and Michelangelos, the Shakespeares and Mozarts, the Renoirs and Rodins, had their deepest roots here in the kingdom of Minos with its Labyrinth and Minotaur, in the soil from which Icarus and Daedalus launched their ill-starred flight, in the world of Dionysus and the oracle at Delphi and Oedipus and Medea. The place where even the adjectives were born.

She stood with Will at the railing and watched the last of the sunset, and now she saw that it was true what they said about sea water in the night—that it fluoresced. Tiny bits of something glowed faintly green as the water churned from beneath the ship. She touched his arm. Will. He was hers now. She had won him. She had done battle and emerged victorious, as always. But the question remained: What would she do with him? Did she really even want him? Or was it just the game, the thrill of the conquest, that torqued her? He was a pretty man. And from what she'd heard, he was not a lowlife, either, not a bum, really, not a grifter, except by choice and by chance, and that was finished now. He had no reason to do those things anymore. He was actually from quite a good family, from some money of his own. He had nearly finished his degree at UVA and could easily go back. Economics, he'd said, to keep his parents happy. And English for him.

It was, of course, far, far, too early to make any decisions, to even be thinking about decisions. Now was a time for simply being, for soaking in, for sensations and sights and, soon, for touches. But still, the question whispered itself: What will you do? Will you take him home with you? The ultimate souvenir? Will you play with him for a time and then dump him alongside the road where you found him? Will you see that he gets back to his own home? Do you even really like him? Could you love him? Does it matter?

She took his hand. He was still terribly upset about Justine's abrupt departure. He didn't know, not really, what had happened to cause that. It was just that detectives came asking questions about her. That they had confiscated her pack but would not say why. That they had searched his pack, too, and asked a lot of things about drugs and crossing borders. That they had searched Darcy's as well and somehow found neither drugs nor the package, which she produced again after they'd left.

Still, it was his decision in the end to leave without Justine. Darcy said she'd stay with him in Athens, but he said he knew that Justine would want him to make the delivery. That was paramount.

He was a little distant, although he let her hold his hand. Maybe he was angry or at least confused. Frightened? Curious? Titillated? Time would tell, and, more important, time would ameliorate. It mattered to get where they were headed and then to hunker down. To begin the real work—on him. To convert him entirely from his worship at the shrine of Justine to sating himself at the pagan feast of Darcy. Then the adventure would really begin.

Galini

Ten

THEY CAME THEN ON A bus over the mountains from Iraklion to stay in the Hotel Papigal at the edge of the village of Agia Galini where a fall of dark boulders ran from the white sea wall down to the narrow rocky beach. In the beginning Darcy could not stop remarking on the coloration of the water, how it turned in bands from blue to green to silver to rust and back to a deeper blue again out at the horizon, although perhaps that last was just the color of the sky reflected in it. How it changed with the weather, too, becoming steely and dark as clouds formed. Will could not stop remarking on how they had to deliver the package even without Justine and how he didn't know where to take it or to whom, and what would happen if they didn't get it delivered?

On the second day when, after Darcy reminded him again that Maurice had said to just wait and someone would find them, and Will seemed to settle some, she paid for them to go out in one of the fishing boats so they could look back at the island and try for a shark or a swordfish. They saw that the deeper blue was not the sky but the water itself. If you looked straight down into it, you could see that it deepened all the way to black, and that was the soul of the sea. She shuddered when she saw it and stepped back away from the railing. The captain and the deckhand laughed, but Will kept staring into it until the line was ready and they had cast it and let it dive and dive into that blackness.

LATE THAT AFTERNOON SHE CALLED Matthew's hotel in Athens.

"Darcy," he said. "What's going on?"

"Not much. How about with you?"

"Well, I talked with the police, who said they'd questioned you and that drugs were involved."

"Oh, my."

"Are you in trouble?"

"No. I called them."

"Yes, that's what they said."

"And didn't you believe them?"

"I'm not sure."

"Do you believe me?"

"I'm not sure."

She laughed. "I just saw a bag with a bunch of stuff in it. That's all."

"Apparently that's not all. It belonged to someone you knew, didn't it?"

"Well, sort of."

"So you turned over this Justine person and then left."

"How do you know about her."

"She has a file, as you can imagine. So does her ex-husband, Maurice Winterbottom. I found a waiter at the American Café in Venice who recognized you from a picture I showed him and remembered seeing you talking to Maurice."

"My, you are thorough."

"These don't seem to be very nice people, Darcy, especially not the sort I'd want to piss off by narcing on them. I'm not sure you know what you've gotten yourself into."

"Not really. Do you?"

"Not yet. But I'm learning."

"Me, too. And I'm peachy, so not to worry."

"Where are you?"

"Ah, ah, ah."

"Please, can we stop this? I've been sitting in this room for two days. It's not very pleasant just waiting."

"Oh, come on. I bet Daddy puts you up in great hotels, doesn't he? Fabbo room service, in-room massages, and all that. But you're an all-work kind of guy, I bet, aren't you, Matthew? No playtime, at least not on a job."

"Are you on Crete yet?"

"Now I am *really* impressed."

"So you are."

"How in the world did you know that? I paid cash—"

"Darcy—"

"No, no. This is part of the fun. You have to tell me."

"I don't think you realize what sort of people these are, this Justine and Maurice."

"You already said that. How did having their names lead you to Crete?"

"There are things you don't know."

"Then *tell* me, Matthew. Come on."

"I don't really know much, either. But Maurice owns real estate there."

"Well, good for Maurice."

"Listen, I've booked a room in Iraklion. The Hotel Anastasia. You can go there now. The room's under both our names. I'll be in tonight."

"I won't be."

"I didn't think you would."

"Anastasia. Pretty name. I guess I'll talk to you after you get here—if you're lucky."

"You mean if *you're* lucky."

"Matthew, you worry too much."

"And you should."

She hung up.

THEIR ROOM WAS NARROW, WITH a cracked red linoleum floor and a bathroom so tiny that to use the handheld shower you had to close the toilet and sit. The room held only two single beds, a small desk, and a bookcase. But it also opened directly onto the beach and had a window wide enough to allow them a view of the southern curve of the coastline that ran away from the town in both directions. And so the sea filled the room, and in the mornings they woke with the first pink light that came over it.

They took to walking in the early mornings. The shore to the west was broken and soon ended at the base of a rough cliff with an olive orchard at its top, but to the east they could pick their way among the rocks, find long stretches of sand, and go for more than an hour sometimes. Later they had breakfast in one of the *tavernas* or *kafenía* along the main street of the village where they took all their meals. Sometimes they had nothing more than tough bread, white butter, and a pot of the tarry, bitter skéto that they had both come to crave.

On the morning of the fourth day, after breakfast, they went into a shop that passed as one of the town's general stores. It held small selections of toiletries, stationery materials, and hardware, and larger ones of touristy trifles, Greek-subtitled videotapes, and groceries. Will was looking for something to read. He was already beginning to seem bored, which Darcy found disconcerting. They had each other to keep them amused and happy and satiated. And she certainly felt all three of those things. Will had proved to be a robust and durable lover, and Darcy did not feel disappointed in him except at the furthest edges of her desires. He was not especially inventive, she thought, or daring. But his enthusiasm made up for it, and the previous days had been a swirl of sensual satisfactions, from Will to the warm ocean to the strange, wonderful foods to the feel of the sun in the days before Christmas. She hoped he wasn't already tiring of this Eden they were in together.

As he browsed a rack of months-old magazines, she wandered down one of the store's two aisles to the rear wall where there hung a display of miniature decorative spoons with various emblems or symbols embossed on the flattened handles. It was something you'd see in an American tourist trap. These had the predictable Greek flag or Greek and American flags intertwined or Greek and British. One, though, said simply *Matala,* and beneath it was an image of what appeared to be a high cliff with pockmarks on its face.

She looked around. There was only the clerk up front behind the counter and Will at the reading rack. She had seen a man stocking shelves when they came in, but he had apparently gone into the back room. She touched one of the other spoons first, a flag one, lifted it and felt its weight, and put it back. She looked around again and then quickly lifted the Matala spoon and palmed it. Another glance, and then she slipped it down the front of her shorts and inside the band of her panties where she had meant it to stay, but it slipped down into her crotch. There was some danger, of course, that it would slip out and clatter to the floor, which would be at the least an embarrassment. But she liked the sensation of the cool metal there. She took a few experimental steps and could feel it moving against her.

The man came out of the back now and looked at her. He smiled. "You like?"

She nodded. "Just looking, though."

He went toward the front. Will seemed to have chosen something, so she wandered up slowly so as not to jar anything and went out and waited for him at the curb of the narrow lane.

When he emerged with a brown paper bag holding several magazines, she took his hand and pulled him in the direction of the hotel.

"What?" he said.

"Just come with me."

When she was thirteen years old, she had gone with her mother to a beauty salon. Her haircut had taken only fifteen minutes, but her mother's perm was going to be at least an hour. She sat reading for a while and then got up and wandered over to the rack of expensive shampoos, conditioners, toners, and dyes, and lifted several to read the labels. The women were farther back, either working or being worked upon, except the one behind the counter who was either terribly engrossed in the article she was reading or asleep. Darcy slipped a small spritzer bottle into her purse. It was not the first time she had stolen something, but she was still new to it.

Later, as she waited for her mother to pay so they could leave, she saw her talking to the woman at the counter, and then the two of them looking at her. Then another woman joined them, listening and nodding and watching her. And then a third woman, older than the others, the owner or manager or something, came up, too. They were all looking at her.

She felt frightened in a way, but excited, too. She remembered even years later the feel of sweat running down her sternum, though the place was overly air-conditioned. She remembered the feel in her gut of hunger and desire, and of the urge it gave her to leap up and run from the store before anyone could do anything. But she did not run. She got up and walked past the women and into one of the bathrooms. She tossed the bottle of hair spray into the trash, then pulled her pants down, sat on the edge of the toilet seat, and touched herself, and almost immediately she came. She couldn't believe it had happened that easily. She had touched herself before, in her bed at night, and had climaxed, but never this easily or this intensely. She felt dizzy and sat breathing for several minutes before washing her hands and going out. Her mother waited at the door. She did not look at the other women as she passed them.

Outside in the sun and heat of a June parking lot afternoon, her mother gripped her upper arm hard enough that Darcy knew she would have a bruise.

"Ow!"

"Shush," her mother said. "What did you do?"

"With what?"

"In that store? What did you take?"

"Nothing. God, Mother, will you let go of me?"

"I had to pay for a bottle of very expensive setting spray that they said was missing after you looked at it."

"That's bullshit."

"You watch your mouth. This isn't the first time, Darcy. I know what you do."

"I don't have anything!" she said. "Just because you think I've done it before, you believe them now over me? Let's go back in there. I'll show you. I don't have any stupid thing of theirs."

"I'll never go in there again. You've ruined that. It was my favorite place, too."

"I don't have anything. Do you want to search me?"

"I want you to get over this," her mother said.

Now, as soon as they entered their Galini hotel room, Darcy grabbed Will and pressed her mouth into his. She held him tightly to her and kissed his neck and chest.

"Darcy," he said.

"Please," she told him. "Right now. Don't talk."

"But I—"

"Please."

He kissed her again, or let her kiss him, and then she felt him at the snaps of her shorts. She felt them fall around her ankles and felt him at the top of her panties and his fingers creeping down in that delicious way, and then he touched the spoon and withdrew.

"What the hell?" he said.

"It's yours," she said. "Take it out. I got it for you."

"What is it?"

"Take it out." She lay down on one of the beds, and he sat beside her and reached in again and pulled out the spoon.

"Did you steal it?"

"Mmm-hmm."

"Why?"

"No reason."

"But—"

"Don't stop," she said. She pulled his hand back to her belly and pushed it down until he bent over her again and kissed her, and soon there was no question of stopping.

THAT NIGHT, AFTER SHARK STEAKS and a liter of the sweet retsina, she told Will she'd meet him back at the room in a few minutes. Then they could decide whether to go to the Korus Club again or somewhere else that night. She went to the pay phone outside the Rent-a-Vespa shop and had to wait for some stupid girl to finish giggling with her boyfriend. The holiday influx had swollen the little town to the point of making it uncomfortable. It had been theirs for a few days, but it was not anymore. When the girl finished, Darcy dialed the Anastasia in Iraklion.

"Darcy," Matthew said, "I'm so glad you called."

"And I'm so glad that you're so glad."

"Listen. It's time to stop screwing around. You may be in trouble."

"Well, there's a news flash."

"I don't mean with your father. I mean danger."

"What kind of danger?"

"Justine and Maurice. We're starting to get some information on them, what they may be involved with."

"Which is?"

"Why did they tell you you were going to Crete?"

"To deliver a package."

"And where is it? The package."

"I have it hidden."

"What's in it?"

"I don't know."

"You haven't looked?"

"No."

"God, Darcy."

"It's not drugs. She told me that."

"It could be anything."

"Such as?"

"Or worse. It could be nothing. Have you thought of that?"

"I don't understand."

"Darcy, look at it. Open it."

"They'll know."

"Fuck them!"

She waited. He was angry now. Not angry—he was frightened. She could hear that. "Matthew," she said, "tell me what you know."

"I don't know anything. I'm just getting bits and pieces of things that don't make sense, but they make me think you may be in great jeopardy."

"Will is with me, you know. He wouldn't let them do anything—"

"Will is involved in it, too, somehow."

"Will? He's clueless."

"He may be clueless, but he's involved. With them. With her—Justine."

"They've been traveling together. They were lovers."

"Before that."

"Before?"

"Long before."

"What— He would've said something."

"If I'm correct, he doesn't know."

"Matthew, I'm really confused."

"Tell me where you are?"

"I'm not ready yet."

"Darcy—"

"I'm in the south. I'll tell you that. I'm not in Iraklion."

"And you're with Will."

"Yes."

"Just the two of you?"

"Yes."

"But they know where you are?"

"This is where she said to come, to this town."

"Where?"

"I'll call you tomorrow. How about that?"

"Are you in Matala?"

"Why would you ask me that?"

"Are you?"

"No, but I saw it on a spoon today."

"Is this another clue?"

"Tomorrow," she said and hung up.

Eleven

On the fifth morning it was still dark when I opened my eyes. The sun had begun to rise, but the sky was heavily overcast and the air felt heavy and dead. It had turned chilly, too. I rested against the cool plaster wall and watched Darcy sleeping in the other bed, one arm flung above her head. Her hair had lightened with the ocean and the sun so that it could be called blond now, a careless sort of blond. She wore nothing because we had made love again after we came in from drinking and then slept together for the first hours of the night, as we had each night, until she woke at some point and went to the other bed. The sheet was pushed down to her waist so that I could make out the hardened nipples, each nestled in the pendentious convexity of its great mother ship, and even some of the definition of the muscles in her arms. She worked out, she told me—aerobics and running and weight lifting. She had a private trainer in Cleveland. She was, it turned out, a rather violently healthy girl.

I thought about what they felt like, those biceps, deltoids, and pectorals, not only their strength and heat but the quality of the darkening skin. It was like a kind of hide. Justine's skin was pale and soft and so tender it burned even in moderate sun.

As I watched, Darcy shifted and made a sound in her throat, then pushed with her legs so that the sheet rode down further, exposing the tangled top of her pubic nest. She turned her head and made another sound, and now I could see her hips moving, just perceptibly, thrusting upward. I wondered if she was dreaming of me or if, maybe, it was the man she had danced with in the bar last night or some other man altogether.

She had a remarkable clitoris, so large and turgid that I had taken to calling it her little penis, which only made her laugh. Justine's thin blade of a one lay in such a deep valley that I had to move the folds of her mons to even glimpse it, like some exposed little treasure. She had liked for me to do that.

I had an erection now, which I regretted. It ached because we had made hard love not too many hours before. Darcy, it seemed, always wanted it that way—simply hard and often. I had tried to be subtle, tried to use some of the small maneuvers, the tiny touches I'd learned from Justine that she loved for me to do, commanded me to do, sometimes for an hour or more before she would let me move on. But they were lost on this girl even when she was sober. "Just *fuck* me," she would say and grasp her ankles, straighten her legs, and tell me, "Harder" or "Faster" or "Deeper." Sometimes, for variety, she said things in French—*"Plus profond!"* or *"Baisez-moi!"*—and once, I believe, something in Italian, though I couldn't really make it out.

Even when I gave up and just tried to pulverize her with my thrusting (thinking that at some point it would be too much), she only cried out for more, and the longer I lasted (it was taking longer and longer the more we did it), the harder and more wetly and more loudly she came. She had surprised me yet again with this newest manifestation of her true nature—and, frankly, shocked me a little, as did the fact that for the first time in the short history of my sex life, I felt weary of it.

I looked away, toward the wide window and the weak light over the southern sea, and thought of what I had done, how I had come to be in this place with this endlessly horny woman, and how we had lost Justine somehow, and of what I might say to her if she ever found me again.

No one had contacted us. Maurice did not seem to be here or any of his people or Justine, and so we just did what we wanted or, anyway, what Darcy wanted, which was to eat and drink and fuck and walk and fuck and maybe swim a little and then fuck.

As the light struggled to rise, I looked at her again and drew in my breath when I saw that she was looking back. She'd pushed the sheet down further so that she was entirely uncovered, and she lay with her legs parted.

"Merry Christmas," she said. "Would you like your present?"

"It's not till tomorrow."

"Oh. Then you still have time to shop."

"As long as it's for a dead fish. Do you want a fish?"

"Mmm. What kind of fish?"

"What kind do you want?"

"One that's shaped like your cock and that tastes like it."

"A cock fish," I said.

"But not just any cock fish. A big old Will-shaped cock fish. Then when you're gone, it can keep me company."

"Where will I be going?"

"I don't know, but we can't stay in this tiny room forever no matter how cheap it is. You'll have to get a job or something someday."

"You're not going to support me?"

"It'd be bad for your self-esteem. Plus, if you never go away, you'll never miss me. You might even get tired of me."

"Will you miss me?"

"Oh, yes. But I'll have your cock fish to help me get by."

"But I might only be gone for a little while."

"It doesn't matter. I can't be without it. I'm obsessed with it. The taste of it. The shape. Having it in me. I could have some right now."

"But you just had some."

"That was hours ago. I told you—I really am insatiable."

"I believe you."

"You like it, don't you?"

"What?"

"My insatiability."

"I'm not complaining."

"But—"

"But nothing. I've just never known a girl quite like you."

"How many girls have you known?"

"Not all that many."

"Well, however many you meet, none will be like me."

"I believe that, too."

"So do you want to?" She spread her legs further and combed the nest with her fingers.

"We could, or we could be good and then reward ourselves later."

"Hmm," she said. "That sounds awfully ascetic and spartan."

I rubbed my face, stretched, sat up, lifted my jeans from the floor, and pulled them on. "Come on," I said. "We can get in a nice walk before it gets warm."

On this morning there were fresh eggs, which there had not been for several days. Darcy ordered them cooked for four minutes, and when the white crockery cups arrived, they came not only with a plate of toast but a thickly oiled slice of feta as well, courtesy of the proprietor. Darcy spread the cheese on the bread and spooned the runny yolk and albumen onto it. She purred at the complex mingling of the flavors.

After she paid, we sat sipping the coffee and watching out the front window over the cobbled street.

"Are you all right?" she asked.

"Mmm."

"You're not talking much."

"Just full," I said. "And tired. All that partying. And that other thing we do."

"I don't have any idea what you mean."

"You seemed interested in that guy at the Korus last night."

"I didn't see you for a while. Where did you go?"

"I picked up some chick and screwed her on the beach."

"Not really."

"I smoked part of a doob with some people."

"And you didn't invite me?"

"Well, you were busy with that guy."

"Because you wouldn't dance. I'd rather have been dancing with you."

I watched her eyes follow someone past the window.

"Did you want to do him?"

She shrugged. "Not especially. I have this guy, see."

"You do?"

"Yeah. He's a pretty great guy."

"In what way?"

"Oh, lots of ways. Except that he teases me about how he picks up strange girls and fucks them on the beach."

"I bet he just says that to make you jealous."

"Why would he want to do that?"

"Because he's insecure, I suppose."

"Insecure? But why? He's got a big old fish, that boy. And he's beautiful. He's got nothing to be insecure about."

"Maybe those aren't the things he's insecure about."

"Well, what then?"

"I don't know. Maybe he doesn't know."

"Hmm," she said. "Are we ready for our reward?"

"We just ate. Shouldn't we digest first?"

"I don't need to."

"I'm tired."

"Then we should go take a nap."

"It's barely past nine."

"We don't have to just sleep."

"Do you really want to?"

"Of course I want to. I always want to."

I nodded. "Are you happy?"

"I love it here," she said. "But do you?"

"I'm just waiting."

"Maybe that's what's wrong. Stop thinking about it. It'll find you when it's ready for you. Until then, just take it in. Just love it."

"I have been. Really, I have."

"Maybe if you don't look for it, it won't come."

"It'll come. Anyway, shall we go take a nap?"

"Only if you'll fuck me."

"I said I was tired."

"You've been up for only three hours. You must have one good fuck in you, no?"

"Maybe when we wake up." I looked at her.

"Are you getting bored with me?"

"I was just thinking how this makes you look. The sun and the ocean work for you. You're darker and your hair's lighter. And you've got those little lines by your eyes when you smile now."

"God, don't tell me that."

"I like them."

"I'm never going outside again."

"Well, maybe they have a cot for you in the back here. You'll probably have to start doing dishes, though."

"Maybe, but I bet I could get a good fuck here."

"Probably quite a few."

When we got up, the waiter smiled and asked if we'd be in for dinner that night. "We have maybe the *koliós,* yes?"

"Mackerel," said Darcy.

"Ah," I said. "How?"

"We do the . . . slice." The waiter drew his hand, palm up, through the air in front of him.

"Filleted."

"*Néh,* yes, on the grill, with haricot beans and vegetables." He said the last word as if it were three.

"Mmm, yes," I said, stroking my chin. "Nice." I nodded, and she laughed and said, "The Galloping Gourmet."

"Or the gutter eater."

She said, "Come on. Let's hurry. I'm ready for dessert."

"You don't have dessert after breakfast."

"You do here."

"Oh, no," I said. "Nap time."

"Just come on," she said, taking my hand and dragging me out into the light.

THAT EVENING, AFTER IT HAD been dark for some time and we had eaten the mackerel and sat after dinner over shots of ouzo and unshelled peanuts, we again walked back to the room. Only the bathroom light was on. Darcy undressed in silence, pulling harshly at her sweater and jeans and throwing them in a ball on the floor.

"I can't believe you're this pissed off," I said. She'd been angry since our mid-morning nap when I did not make love to her either before or after.

Still, she did not speak but unsnapped her bra, threw it on the bed, and pulled her panties off, too. The room was chilly and her nipples puckered, and even in the dim light I could see goose bumps along her arms and legs.

"Do you think I don't want you anymore? Do you think I don't find you attractive? I'm just tired. All I said was can't we give it a rest for a day?"

She looked at me, letting me take in her nakedness, then took a shortish black dress from a hanger. It was chilly outside now. It was December, after all, and even here in the Mediterranean the winds came at night and dropped the temperature down sometimes into the forties. But where we were going wasn't more than fifty yards from the room, and it would be very warm there.

"Okay," I said. "Fine. Let's do it. But can we try something different, maybe? A different position?"

"I told you, I can't come that way."

"What way? We haven't tried it yet."

"I've tried other ways. It's not like you're my first guy."

"No kidding."

"And they never work."

"Well, maybe there are some ways you haven't tried. Or the guys you tried them with weren't any good."

"Flatter yourself."

"No, I'm just saying."

"I don't like it other ways."

"Whatever," I said and began to undress.

She pulled the dress on over her head.

"So why are you getting dressed?"

She looked at me and said, "I'm not giving you anything. From now on if you want it, you'll have to take it."

"What?"

"You'll have to take it. No more easy street."

"Easy street? Who the fuck says that?"

She pretended to ignore me. She said, "Hmm-mm-mm, here I am, just a single girl getting dressed for Christmas Eve. All alone in her room. No men anywhere." Then she looked at me and widened her eyes. "Oh, my God! Who are you? How did you get in here?"

"Darcy," I said. "Hello?"

"Were you watching me get dressed? You pervert. You sicko."

She had her arms crossed in an X over her breasts, as if the dress weren't enough to shield them.

"What are we doing?" I asked.

"I'm going to call the police," she said, "if you don't get out of here. Don't you touch me." She stepped toward me.

"Darcy." When I put a hand on her arm, she acted as if I'd pushed her and fell back onto the bed.

"You son of a— I know what you're here for. Don't you dare try it." The dress had ridden up or she'd pulled it up so that she was exposed now from the belly down.

"Is this the something different?"

"Freak," she said.

"Listen—" I recognized the game.

"Monster," she said.

I sat beside her. "Do you like it like this?" I put my hands on her shoulders and held her, and she made a show of trying to push me away.

"Don't . . . you . . . *dare.*"

"Is this really what you like? Will you just tell me?" It was in a way a version of Justine's game, only the converse of it.

"Asshole."

"Bitch."

"Freak."

"Weirdo."

"Fuck you."

"Fuck *you.*" How strange that in a sense I had two women, and both had this need of control—one to exercise it and one to be subjected to it.

"Try it."

I kissed her then, pushing my face to hers even though she pretended to try to turn away, and when I touched her legs, she pressed them together.

"No!" she said when I got a knee between her knees. "No!" She was getting loud now, and I worried that someone might hear and actually call the police.

"Darcy," I said.

"Get off me!"

And in spite of myself, I felt it turn me on, felt myself harden as I forced her legs apart and pinned her arms and reached down to undo my jeans. And for a moment, I believe, I felt what Justine felt, what beguiled her so. This power over someone, sexual power, this act of quasi-raping plucked some chord that was so deep, so ancient and primal that one could hardly sense it, let alone name it. But it was there.

But that feeling, which I was suspicious of anyway, evaporated when Darcy hit me. I thought later that she'd just meant it as a movie slap, a loud crack on the cheek, but I'd somehow moved so that the heel of her hand split my lower lip badly enough that I was immediately bleeding onto her.

"Ah," I said and sat back and held it.

"Serves you right."

"Darcy! For Christ's sake."

"I can feel your big animal cock," she said and thrust up against me.

"Fuck it," I said and got off her. This wasn't Justine binding me for pleasure. This just hurt. "Fuck the whole thing. You're nuts."

"Sissy," she said. "Chicken shit. Big man afraid of a little girl slap. Can't get it up?"

"Shut *up,*" I said, leaning into her face. I held one of my T-shirts against my mouth. "Just shut . . . the fuck . . . up."

She looked at me and said, "Big baby."

That was when I left.

THE KORUS CLUB WAS LITTLE more than a glassed-in beach room with a bar, some garden tables, and a mediocre sound system. It had a sour, moldy odor that tended to fade as the night went on. In addition to beer and ouzo, it had some better liquors that still weren't very expensive. And as the holiday had neared, the town began to fill up with travelers, students from Continental or English universities on their winter breaks, and Americans, Australians, and Canadians on longer journeys, come for the relative warmth and sun. On a good bright day, if you had a bit of a constitution, you could swim for a while in the ocean and enjoy it. It wasn't hot, but it wasn't winter, either. These newcomers rented rooms, ate the cheap food, and got drunk every night, and the Korus Club was really the only place to be, so now, on this eve of Christmas, it was wall-to-wall already by nine o'clock.

I didn't care. I tried to ignore it. I sat at the bar, sipping on a Czech Bud and nursing a neat Dewars that I dipped my lip into every now and then. I hadn't been there twenty minutes when someone sat down beside me. I was afraid it was Darcy, so I didn't look.

"Hey, mate. Bitch problems?"

Now I looked and gave a start. I looked around. "Where—"

"I mean, look at that," Maurice said and held out his hand to show the ugly half-healed burn on his palm. "Bleedin' wenches, all of 'em."

"When did you get here?"

"Relax, son," Maurice said. "You're all right." On the next stool over sat a large ugly man I had not seen before.

"That's Karl," said Maurice.

Karl did not look up from his drink.

"Where's Justine? Have you seen her?"

"Shhh," Maurice said. "Just listen to me. Do you know what happened to her?"

"No."

"No idea?"

"These cops were asking about her, where she was, how I knew her, all that. They'd torn all her stuff apart. I just kind of bullshitted 'em."

Maurice nodded, lit a cigarette, and offered me one.

"No, thanks. They'd brought my pack down and gone through it, too, but didn't find anything. We had that stuff, you know—"

"Right—"

"But the girl, Darcy? Remember her?"

"Oh, yeah."

"She'd taken it. She was holding it, so I was clean."

"Good thing. They didn't rifle her bag?"

"Yeah, but they didn't find anything. Not the package, either."

"Hmm."

"And Justine was out there, across the street. I signaled so she'd know."

"Good lad," Maurice said. "Very smart."

"What happened?"

"You really don't know?"

"No."

"This girl, the one you been shagging the shit out of all week—"

"How do you—"

"Shh. She set her up, mate. She planted the shit in Justine's pack and called the narcs. Claimed Justine was trying to sell them to her."

"Oh," I said. I felt dizzy for a moment. "I haven't seen the package. She had it—"

Maurice nodded. "Not especially worried about it. Where she goes, it goes, you know?"

"Yeah. I hope. What is it?"

"You don't know that, either?"

"No."

"You don't know much, do you?"

I shook my head and said, "I'd rather not, really."

Maurice laughed, and I felt a little better. Maybe they wouldn't kill me or even beat the shit out of me. I'd never felt comfortable around Maurice even when we were smoking the O. Something about the way he looked at you, like he was just waiting for you to make a slip so that then he could own you. And, of course, Justine had told me stories of what Maurice and his men had done to those who'd crossed him.

"Funny, funny boy," Maurice said. "I can see what she sees in you. Don't know what you see in her. Well, that's not true. But that's not for now."

"So what is it?"

"Oh, you might say it's an icon."

"A what?"

"Icon. A figurine. You know, the female form and all that."

"You mean like a statue? A sculpture?"

"Something like that."

"That valuable, huh?"

"A steamin' fortune."

"You stole it?"

"I didn't. Someone did, in a manner of speaking. I just make the connections, such as they are."

"And you get a fee."

"Now you're gettin' it."

"I looked in her pack when she was sleeping a few days ago, and I didn't see it there. I don't know where it is. I really don't. I wish I did, Maurice. I'd tell you. I'd rather you had it than her."

"I believe that," Maurice said. "Not to worry, as I said. But I am gonna have to take you with me, you know."

"Take me?"

"Just think of it as a party, lad. We'll go on up to my house."

"What house?"

"She never told you I had a house here?"

"No."

"Oh, yeah. Nice one. Over in Matala." He leaned in, lowered his voice, and said, "Got a pipe and a couple balls of O up there, too. Interested? How long since you've done that?"

"A while."

"All right then." He straightened up and said, "Yeah, I've had this place for years. She lived there, too, once. Can't believe she never mentioned it."

"She didn't."

"Well, yes, I can—believe it, I mean. You got a lot to learn, son, starting with don't ever get involved with two women at the same time when one of them is named Justine."

Karl laughed, the first sound he'd made, a single *harrgh* down into his drink.

"Right, then," said Maurice. "Let's take a ride."

Twelve

WHEN JUSTINE OPENED THE DOOR of the little hotel room and stepped inside, Little Bitch was lying on the bed, presumably where Will had left her, staring at the ceiling. She had on a black dress, and it was hiked up to her waist so that little cunny was hanging out.

"Came back for more?" the girl said. "You need it as much as I do, don't you, lover?"

"I do," said Justine.

"Oh!" The girl scrambled up and covered herself. "Shit." She grabbed a pillow and held it over her chest as if it would protect her. "What the fuck!" she said. "What are you doing? You just walk in?"

"I do, yes, dear. I just walk in." Justine set down the nylon bag she was carrying, locked the door behind her, turned around the desk chair, and sat down.

"Get out of here." Darcy sat curled into herself, against the wall.

"Or what?"

"I'll scream."

"Oh, you may well scream, but I'm not leaving."

"Someone will come."

"Only me. This is a small town. The people who enforce the laws and the people who run the hotels are friendly and open to persuasion, especially when you've been around for a while. I used to live here. Maurice still does, some of the time. He has a house not too far away, at Matala. And he's very generous. They love him. So when he asks a favor—like, oh, say, 'If you hear some screaming coming from a certain room down by the beach, ignore it, will you?'—they're only too happy to go along. Besides, it's not as if there haven't been some pretty provocative sounds coming out of here the past few days. People are used to it by now. You and the boyfriend have developed a bit of a reputation, in case you didn't know. And you might think about closing the drapes now and then."

"Maurice is here?"

"He brought me here. I had to call him from Athens. Collect. All I had were the clothes I was wearing. But you know that."

The girl lowered the pillow and sat up a little straighter on the bed. "I'm sorry—"

"Oh, don't even bother. We both know better."

"Where . . . I mean, what happened?"

"It was a mess, that's what. We only got in here yesterday morning."

"Why didn't you—"

"We were watching. We each had our reasons. He was really of the mind that we didn't need to disturb you if it wasn't necessary. He can be surprisingly thoughtful. I, on the other hand, am not nearly so nice. I was just watching out of a kind of prurient interest—and because, as angry as I was already, I thought I could build on it a little more, you know. Really get up a head of steam. And I've got one."

"Will will come back here."

Justine shook her head. "He's with Maurice."

"Whatever you're going to do—I can get you so much money." Darcy laid the pillow aside, swung her legs over the side of the bed, and looked levelly at Justine.

"I don't want your daddy's money."

"You don't even know how much."

"Nor do I care."

"You did. You sure cared a lot in Rome. You couldn't wait to get your hands on it."

"Well, that was a long, long time ago, wasn't it? I think we all had different priorities then. Amazing what ten days can do."

"Shit."

"You're not swearing in French. Have you noticed that? It happens when you're under stress. Funny how that works. Veneers—and how they fail. How the real person shows through sooner or later."

Darcy shook her head and looked at the floor.

"Oh, come now. You know exactly what I mean. From the first, I felt it. This . . . recognition. You know how you feel that with someone sometimes? Your whole life can go to ruin because of it, but still you have to let it happen. That sort of thing—recognition, reunion, vibe, whatever—it doesn't happen so often. It's quite remarkable, startling, don't you think?"

"I don't know what you're talking about."

"You're just not letting yourself admit it, but it drove you as much as it did me, all the way here."

"I didn't come here because of you."

"Well, yes, you did."

"I did not."

"Then why did you?"

"Because of Will."

"But I told him to come here. I told you both."

"I was just going to go. To have a trip, you know. To just not be bored. And to be with him."

"It goes back further than that—all the way to Rome. When you came with us, you knew we were never going to deliver you to your little group in Florence."

"I did not."

"Yes, you did. In your heart you knew it, and you prayed that you were right."

"You're full of shit."

"*Merde* is a much nicer word. You really should go back to it. Even before that, though, you knew. You knew the wine was wrong, didn't you?"

"What?"

"It must've tasted funny, and it didn't look right. Bit of a bluish cast to it, no? I know you noticed. I saw you. I was so far in your head that night, I might as well have been fucking your brain."

"You're crazy."

"Well, not yet."

"You don't know anything about my head."

"Oh, I do, little girl. More than you could imagine. Far more than you know about yourself."

Justine stood, went over to the bed, and sat down. The girl pushed herself back against the wall again, into the corner, clutched the pillow, and said, "Get away!"

"Shh, pussy. Listen."

She looked up and said, "What?"

"I'm going to hurt you."

"What?"

"In ways you've never imagined. Because you see, even though you've been a monstrous pain in my ass and you're an ungrateful, spoiled, nasty girl, and you stole away my boy and acted like a little whore, any one of which would be reason for me to just cut your pretty throat and have you dumped in the sea, I am going to give you what you've been wanting for so long you can't even remember when it began."

She reached up and lifted a lock of the girl's hair and let it slide through her fingers. The girl couldn't push herself any farther back. She turned her head from one side to the other, trying to keep the hand away. And when she reached up with her own hand to move Justine's, Justine slapped it hard enough that the crack echoed from the plaster walls and the girl shrieked.

"You see?" Justine said.

"What the *fuck—*"

"It'll be easier for us both if you relax. Really. You're not going anywhere. You're mine till sunrise, so you might as well make the best of it. I have a bottle of good English gin in that bag, along with my toys. Would you care for a drink?"

"Yours till sunrise for what?"

"For me to beat you."

"Is this your sick revenge?"

"Not at all. I've been thinking about it ever since I saw you. Disciplining your lovely ass."

"But *why?*"

"Well, because it's what I do. It's how I take my own pleasure from the world. Ask your boyfriend, if you ever see him again, about some of the scenes we put on. Mmm. He's a natural submissive. He responds to power, surrenders to it—as did Maurice. Many do. It makes them comfortable. Makes them feel as if the world is an ordered place."

Darcy covered her face and breathed, then said, "What happens at sunrise?"

"We deliver the package."

"I cut it open. There's nothing in it but newspaper."

"Well, then, I guess that's not the package after all, is it?"

"It's me," the girl said. "Isn't it?"

Justine smiled.

With a cry, Little Bitch leaped at her. With fingers arched and claws extruded, she went for the eyes. But Justine had been waiting for it. She swung her arms and deflected the thrust so that Little Bitch fell off the bed, and then Justine was on her. The girl was stronger, there was no doubt, but these things were never about physical strength.

Justine held her against the cool floor. "Shh. Listen, pussy. Maybe I'm wrong about you, but I don't think so. And if I'm not wrong, then you know it. You just have to let yourself accept it. Let yourself have what you've been looking for for so long. It's why you steal, you know. You want to be corrected, but no one ever has—not really. And it's left you unmoored, floating. I can take that away, but only if you'll let me."

The girl was crying now. Justine felt her let go, when she finally saw how it was going to be. She was not stupid. She was frighteningly bright, really. Justine had known that. But there was something else behind it now, too—a kind of peace. That did not come as a surprise.

Justine said, "That's better, isn't it? You know who I am. You know how happy you can be. Join the world already. It's a wonderful place."

The girl was quiet another moment, then she said, "I think I will have a drink."

"Of course you will. Come." Justine stood and helped the girl back onto the bed. "I'm afraid we'll have to do without ice, uncivilized as that is, but I did manage to find a lime."

"That's fine."

They drank in silence, quickly, with a purpose. The gin was smooth and the lime tart, and it went down well. And then Justine set the glasses aside and leaned forward until she could feel Little Bitch's breath on her face, could smell the gin and lime, and under that the fish she'd had for dinner and the horrible Greek excuse for liqueur. Justine licked her face. And licked her face again, up one cheek to the pretty eye and across and down the other.

And then the girl, finally knowing that she was home, could only say, "Oh, God," and their mouths were each upon the other. And then Justine took hold of the front of the little black dress with both her hands, pulled until it ripped, and tore it all away. And as her tongue searched the girl's mouth, she took her nipples between her fingernails.

"Such tits," she whispered, and then she pinched. The girl's mouth opened all the way when she screamed so that Justine could now explore its very depths.

IN THE MORNING, WHEN THE first threads of light wove themselves through the darkness, Justine shook her and said, "Come. It's time to quit this dump."

"Mmm," the girl said. She had fallen asleep minutes earlier, her head on Justine's thigh.

"Come, love."

"Where?"

"We have to deliver the package."

"Let's just run away."

Justine said, "Mmm. You are just a silly little bitch, aren't you?" And she kissed her.

"Please," the girl said.

"Shh."

"Please don't. Please."

Justine felt hot tears running down between her legs. She said, "Shh. You'll be fine. I'll help you."

The girl went into the bathroom to dress and stuffed her clothing into her new red backpack. They went outside into the dim dawn to find Karl waiting in Maurice's ancient Mercedes 600 saloon. She helped the girl into the back, sat beside her, and held her as they drove through the quiet town toward the hills and the pass that led to Matala.

Matala

Thirteen

DARCY SETTLED INTO THE OLD cool leather and pressed herself against Justine. She did not want to be away from her, to be parted from her even by the space of a backseat. Justine lifted her arm and laid it over Darcy's shoulders.

"Please," Darcy said.

"Shh. Quiet, pussy."

The road was new and wide and black, and followed the shoreline at first. When it turned into the mountains, it rose steeply, and Karl dropped into a lower gear. The engine whined, and they could feel the vibration of the strain. The breeze through the partially opened window was warm, and Darcy smelled the sea and the Greek mountain air, and imagined how old this place was, how long there had been people here. Her head grew light with the thoughts of it. Then she closed her eyes, let her head fall back against Justine, and breathed in her smell as well, and everything still seemed possible.

"Tell me something," Justine said. "When did you open the package?"

"Yesterday."

"Why didn't you look sooner? I don't understand that. I'd have looked as soon as possible to at least know what the game was." She was quiet and then said, "I hoped you'd look. Then maybe you wouldn't have come all the way here."

"I probably still would have."

"Why?"

"I don't know."

"When you found it was empty, why didn't you run?"

Darcy shrugged. "What's the difference?"

"You're a stupid girl," said Justine. "I wanted you to come. I wanted to have last night. I've dreamt of that. But I didn't want you to. I wanted to think of you out there somewhere. Running. Stealing. Doing what you do." She began to cry a little, for the second time in the few days that Darcy had been with her.

Darcy reached up, touched her wet cheek, and tasted the tears. "We can still go, you know."

Justine shook her head.

After they had climbed for some time, the road turned back to cobbles and they came to a small village. They found themselves in the midst of a procession of some kind, with the men in black and white and the women and children following. Darcy thought at first it was a funeral, but there was no casket. Then she remembered it was Christmas morning. The children stared at them. The street in the town was so narrow and Karl had to pull so far over that she could have reached through the window and run her fingers along the rough façades of the whitewashed houses.

"Tell me why," Darcy said. She touched Justine's hair, held it, pressed it to her nose.

"Just money."

"Stupid old money. But you said you didn't care about it anymore."

"No. I said I didn't want your father's money."

Justine had stopped crying, but her cheeks were red with the wind and the wetness.

Darcy felt a heaviness in her belly, the near sickness of mortal fear, but she also felt a calm she had not felt in a long time. She didn't know exactly what was planned for her, but she found that she didn't care—at least about the details. It would be bad if it happened, and that was all she really needed to know. Even without looking in the package, she had known since Athens that something was wrong in all this, as Matthew had known. But this was not the end of the game, though it was the beginning of the end. She was excited for it to play out but was rendered nearly numb at the real possibility that it could end very badly for her. And yet she felt composed. She was as good as Justine at all this. She knew she was now, and soon Justine would know as well. Perhaps it would turn out that she would not win. But Justine would know. Perhaps, she thought, neither of them would win. In a way, that would be best.

After the village, the road immediately began to fall. Karl let it go, and Darcy felt her stomach rise as they dropped faster and faster until she knew that if he erred at all, they'd go over the edge. But she trusted completely in his sense of machines and mechanics and of controlled falling. She had never met him before, but she knew that he was very good at this.

At one point the road leveled out, and they passed along a high chain-link fence with rolled razor wire at the top and then a sign saying that it was a United States military establishment and the taking of photographs in the area was strictly prohibited.

Then they were dropping again. Justine hugged her tightly and leaned with her into the curves. Soon they were down, and the trees opened up and there was the sea again before them. Darcy felt as though they'd arrived at something she knew.

Darcy tapped Justine's leg and pointed at the high red cliffs. Even from that distance she could make out the rows of black openings. "What is it?" she said.

"You don't know about this place?"

"I saw it on a spoon."

"Those are caves hewn into the sandstone. People have lived in them on and off for thousands of years. They were used as crypts, too. In the sixties, people lived there until they were forced out. That's all outlawed now."

"We could live there."

"Don't," Justine said. "You'll only make it harder."

"On who? Me or you?"

Justine did not answer.

They came to a small dirt parking area in a dense copse of cypress and evergreens at one side of the great arena formed by the cliffs and the sand running away toward the ocean. Karl shut off the car. He did not move or speak. Justine helped Darcy out and went around to the trunk. As Darcy stood beside the saloon, she looked back along the dusty road they'd come down. Another Mercedes, a new white one, was moving along slowly in their direction. Darcy looked at it for a long moment and then turned as Justine handed her her things. Justine was carrying the duffel. Darcy put her pack over one shoulder and her purse over the other, and slipped her arm through Justine's. They followed a narrow trail that led through the trees toward the hidden beach. When they came out, the caves were so close that she could see into the lower ones. There was something as ancient, as permanent looking about them as anything she had seen. Though they had clearly been made by men, they seemed as much a part of the landscape as the cliffs themselves or the mountains that formed the center of the island. She felt a strange, almost foreboding quiver when she looked into them. It was as if she could smell the smoke of the fires that had burned there or the odors of the people who had lived in them or the decay of the bodies that had been entombed.

They walked beneath the face toward the water. The small town lay to the south along the beach, and a lower outcropping rose immediately behind it, with houses climbing partway up its face. Several boats were moored just beyond the opening of the cove, and a little way beyond them lay a very large yacht. A hundred and fifty feet, Darcy guessed. Her father had a boat on Lake Erie, a forty-footer that they took to Sandusky or Put-in-Bay or Pelee Island, but he talked often and hungrily of the big boys that went out through the seaway to the ocean. It wasn't that he couldn't have afforded one. It was just that he knew he'd never have the time to make those kinds of trips.

Justine looked out across the cove, then said, "We have a little time. Would you like a drink?"

"A blue one? No, thanks."

Darcy felt dizzy at the thought that it had come to this and how it might still turn out—how a man must feel on death row, on the evening of his execution. A kind of deadness in itself. An unreality.

A walk in the Roman sun, a little respite, and now she might be gone.

"You're strong," Justine said. "Don't ever let that go."

"That's it? I don't want to be strong. I've always been strong—until you, because of you. And I'm supposed to just let that go because you need some cash? How do you think that makes me feel?"

"I don't know," Justine said. "I haven't thought about it."

"Yes, you have. You thought about it all the way here. Even when you hated me, even when I was horrible and ruining your life, I bet it was the only thing you could think of."

"I've never thought you were horrible."

"I was, though."

Darcy hugged Justine's arm, pressed her lips against her ear, and said, "Be selfish. One time in your life, do something just for you. Keep me."

"Please. Stop."

"I won't. Would you let someone do this to you?"

"But you're not me, not remotely."

I am not you, Darcy thought, but I am your equal. And you know it. And if you think this is the end of it, then you've slipped from what you must once have been. But I don't think you've slipped. I think you know.

"No," Darcy said, "I'm not you. I'm yours. *Siete la mia madre.*"

"The real question," Justine said, "is would I let someone do it to you?"

Fourteen

I WOKE EARLY, JUST AT DAWN, as I had each morning on the island. I had not felt like taking the pipe when we got to Maurice's house the night before. It had stopped sounding good to me, especially when I saw that other partiers were already here—two couples who were apparently friendly enough with Maurice that they felt comfortable letting themselves in and digging into his stash. Maurice didn't seem to mind. I had another beer and fell asleep in a room off the kitchen.

I put a kettle on the propane stove, and as I sat at the counter waiting for it to boil, I looked around the place. It was just a small cottage, really, with stuccoed walls, bare wood floors, and fixtures that had obviously been here when Maurice bought it. When the water was hot, I made myself a mug of tea and went into the main room, where Maurice was still sitting on the couch, awake and looking at me. One of the couples was there, too, asleep on a love seat.

"What're you doing?" I asked.

"Christ," Maurice said. "They brought a couple of grams of the marching powder. Can't sleep on that."

He offered me a cigarette, which I accepted. We smoked without speaking for a few minutes, then I made Maurice a cup and we moved out onto the plant-choked veranda. The cottage was at the edge of the town and above most of it. It clung to the lower slope of the hills, which formed the southern wall of the natural amphitheater that embraced the town and the beach and a small blue cove that was so perfectly formed, so perfectly charming, it almost made me laugh. Across from us, forming the northern wall, were the sandstone faces into which the famous caves had been cut millennia before. We smoked and sipped and looked out. Beyond the confines of the cove, out in the open bay, fishing boats and a few larger craft dotted the surface. The air was so clear that I could make out Galini, far up and around the westward curve in the coast.

"So where are they?" I said. "I thought they were coming here."

"Did I say that?"

"Didn't you?"

"Don't think so."

I dragged on the cigarette and stubbed it out. "Well, are they?"

"Justine should be around in a bit."

"And Darcy?"

"I don't know, lad."

"What do you mean? What happened last night?"

"I don't know. I was here, wasn't I?"

"But you knew."

"Why would I?"

"Maurice, quit fucking around."

Maurice looked at me. I saw a chill come into him and then fade. I felt that chill myself. Maurice was an old, strung-out, hopheaded waste of breath, and the man who'd been with him in the bar didn't seem to be around.

"I want to know where she is."

"Lad—" Maurice said.

"Just fucking tell me."

"You'll regret it."

"I don't care."

He looked at his wristwatch and then out across the rooftops at the beach. "She's probably still down there somewhere—for a few more minutes at least." Maurice dragged on the cigarette and looked into the sky. "A place like this don't come easy," he said. "You know? Even when I bought this years ago, it came dear. Foreign taxes, palms to grease, licenses, fees, permits. And then the cost of the place itself. I bought it from a recording engineer, another Brit. He'd had some success. He's the one who built it."

"The point?"

"Takes a lot of money."

"So?"

"Well, I found a business some time ago that made a lot for me. Still does, now and then. Not the most savory business."

"Which is what? Drugs?"

Maurice laughed. "That shit's for wankers. I only handle the stuff so I can own people. It works wonders in that regard. They get so caught up in it, some of them, that they can't leave it. Can't leave you. And you have them then. That's one way."

"What does that mean?"

"There are people in the world who are property, Will. That's what it means. And there are other people who own them." Maurice made a face, finished his cigarette, and flipped it over the railing.

"I don't know what you're talking about, Maurice."

"People own other people. Sometimes it's just an emotional thing. Sometimes it's a need they can't ever leave. And sometimes, Will, people buy other people—for a whole variety of reasons."

"Are you talking about slavery?"

"You could call it that, but it don't tell you much. I mean there are all kinds of slaves, aren't there? Slaves for work, sex, transportation, companionship. And beyond that, there are other sorts of people that people want to buy. Children, for example. People want children and sometimes can't get them, so they buy. But whatever their reason, whatever sort of person they want to own, they need a broker, a finder. Someone to do the dirty work and the moving about and the covering up and the handling of funds and all the thousand shitty little details that go along with it."

"And that's what you do?"

"That's what I do. And it's what Justine did for many years, and she was very good at it."

"And me?"

"You were her first, Will. You were different. You belonged to her in a way none of the others ever did. You were family."

As I looked at him, I felt the drafts rising up the face of the cliff as they'd warmed on the sand, and I could hear them moving in the scrubby trees.

"Your mum was her mum's cousin or something like that. It was fairly distant. But your mum and Justine were about the same age and had come up together. And she was, your mum, something of a fuckup. Knocked up, smacked up, strung out. The whole family wasn't much better. Her people, your people, were grovelers. Shit bags all. Scum of the earth. Justine's mum was gone more'n she was about, and her dad was dead. And then your mum squeezed you out and left as well, and somehow Justine, at the tender age of seventeen or so, had this wee one to deal with. What was she going to do with a naffin' baby? She had no money. But she couldn't see turning it over to the authorities. They'd likely shove you someplace as bad or worse as what you come from, and she'd be left with fuck-all. Anyway, she wasn't your mum, so she had no real authority. So she kept on with it, with you, for some time.

"It happened that I'd had a bit of a hand in this sort of thing, so when she started asking about, someone steered her to me. I, in turn, knew a man in London who knew other people, and so on, who knew a family of Americans who were desperate for a child. It further happened that they were living near London at the time. He was with the foreign service. Deputy attaché or some such. High up. And the long and short of it, Will, is that I put together a deal, laid it out for Justine, and she sold you. And for some flippin' nice coin, I might say."

I stood up and went to the railing at the edge of the veranda and looked down at the rooftops. I suddenly felt ill and was afraid I would be sick, except that some part of me had known this before Maurice said it. Not this, of course, but something. How similar we were, how we looked, how attached we were from the moment she sat next to me in a bar in Roanoke and offered to buy me a beer. It was something between us, some unmistakable bond. I had taken it for love, and as it turned out, I had not been wrong.

"So why did she find me?"

"She missed you, boy. She'd missed you since the day she handed you over. She regretted it. It took her twenty years to come around, but she did. She had left the business by then, and I think that was part of it. It was some small redress for all the souls she bartered, to get back the one she never should have."

"So why . . ." I began but trailed off. I knew now. I knew what it was all about. I felt a wave of nausea again, much worse than the first, but still I did not succumb to it.

"This is all about Darcy, isn't it? She's the package."

"Well, it's not some piece of junk wrapped up in brown paper, is it?"

"Where's she going?"

"Don't know exactly, but it'll be mad hot there."

"You don't even know who bought her?"

"I often don't. In this case, I understand it was one of the wives of some dune coon who actually placed the order. The girl's to be a Christmas present. New toy for the old man and whoever else he wants to invite over to play with it. I mean, what d'you buy for someone that stinkin'? It just worked out, you know. It does that sometimes. Girl shows up with you. Justine feels a connection. That was always her great strength, what made her different. She connected. 'Course it's also what made it impossible for her to stay in. Couldn't take no more.

"Anyway, she called me. I knew of some open orders. They float around. This one was particularly rich, and they were in a bit of a jam because it was fairly specific and time was getting short. So you brought her to Venice where I could see her, and so could they."

"What?"

"You shocked? Anyway, she was perfect. A healthy, bright-eyed, big bapped American girl. It had to be an American. Some of them like it that way. Then, when they're fucking 'em, they feel like they're fucking the whole place, you know?"

"But why did Justine?"

"Sixty thousand quid, split three ways. Less your debts, of course. I didn't like that bit at first. It's always been fifty-fifty. But she insisted. So you're wadded up now, mate."

"I don't want it."

"You will," Maurice said. "You'll want to go off on some quixotic quest to find her. And you'll need lots of folding for that, son. It's how the world works." He pointed to a ship that had anchored just beyond the opening of the cove. "That's her ride. Nice, in'it?"

"Shit," I said and broke for the door, but Maurice was up just as quickly and had me by the arm and the throat.

"Don't think you're gonna cock this up, lad."

"You're sick."

"Greedy, perhaps. Not sick. Now sit down."

"I'm going down there."

"To do what? Karl's there. He's armed. The men coming in are surely armed. And you're going to show up with what, your limp noodle?" He laughed. "It's over. It's done. Now sit down."

He shoved me so that I stumbled back and fell into one of the deck chairs.

"You're a worthless shit, Maurice. She doesn't deserve this. No one does."

"Deserve? What does that mean?"

The mug sat on the small table where I'd set it when it was empty. It was a heavy mug; it felt like clay. I threw it. I didn't think, and that is what's required at certain times. No aiming. No contemplation. Just a reaction. Let the old eye-hand have its way.

The mug hit Maurice square in the face, and I saw blood. Maurice put his hands up, fell to his knees, and gagged. It sounded like gagging anyway. I didn't stay around to hear much of it. I leaped over the wooden railing into the mass of greenery and found myself suspended in the mesh of branches and vines that had not been pruned for forever. As I thrashed, the dry, stiff foliage cut me, especially on the arms. But I was angry and pumped up enough that I hardly cared, and after a few helpless moments, I felt myself dropping and then sliding down the steep rocky slope into the town.

Fifteen

JUSTINE WATCHED TWO MEN CLIMB down the ladder of the yacht into a low fast-looking boat moored at its side. The throaty engine coughed and started, and the boat came toward the beach.

The girl was watching, too. "You asked the question," she said. "Are you going to answer it?" She gripped Justine's shirt. Then she let go, knelt on the sand, and leaned her head against Justine's thighs. "We could be so good," the girl said. "So perfect. You and me. I would obey you."

"What about Will?"

"Will's tired. He needs to go home, get on with things. Don't you think? He needs to get away from you—and me."

Justine looked down at the girl. She couldn't know half the truth, but she was right. It had been good with Will. Good for him and for her. She'd needed to find him. She hadn't realized how much, and she hadn't known what to expect. She never planned on things going nearly as far as they had, on its becoming so involved, but it was so sweet in the beginning. Her baby boy.

"What is he to you really?" the girl asked.

"I knew him when he was a baby. I took care of him."

"Are you related?"

"Yes."

She nodded, the wise girl, and showed no surprise whatever. "I thought it was something. Does he know?"

"Not that I know of."

The boat neared the beach at a fairly high speed so that when the pilot cut the engine, it coasted to the sand and up onto it. The two men on it wore suits. They climbed out and began to walk up the beach toward the women. One of them carried an attaché case.

The girl remained on her knees, head bowed now, as if she were some queen on the block, waiting for the headsman. The men had come close enough for Justine to see that one had very dark skin, black hair, and a thick mustache and the other was lighter and clean-shaven.

Someone shouted from the other end of the beach. It was Will, running toward them.

"Oh, good Christ," Justine said. In that moment she felt things coalesce in some way—or release. Perhaps that was it. They released. She felt things leave her and other things stay. To Little Bitch she said, "Get up."

"For what?" the girl said. "So you can sacrifice me?"

"Just get the hell up."

"Not until you answer the question."

"Oh, Jesus, Mary, and Joseph, Darcy. I wouldn't. I can't. Is that what you want to hear?"

"It doesn't matter what I *want* to hear."

"Well, it's the truth."

She looked up. "You called me Darcy."

"Will you just shut your pretty mouth and come the fuck on."

"Then what?"

"What do you want?"

"Well, I'd like not to be sold."

"Beyond that. You up for another game?"

"I am. Absolutely."

"It's risky."

"Isn't it always?"

"I suppose it is. Let me see your purse."

The girl stood up. Will had reached them now, panting, and the men were steps away.

"Darcy," Will said, "get out of here. They're kidnapping you."

"No," she said. "I've been sold to them."

"What? Get out of here!"

Justine nodded as the men approached and reached for the case, but Will ran at the man holding it and shoved him. "Go!" he shouted at the girl. The man dropped the case and punched him in the stomach, doubling him over, and pushed him to the ground. The other man, the lighter-skinned one, the one who had not carried the briefcase, pulled a small revolver from beneath his suit jacket and held it down at his side so that it was not conspicuous but so that they could see it. He placed his other hand on Darcy's arm. The first man looked at Will a second and then bent and picked up the case. He was about to hand it to Justine when, from the tree line at the head of the beach, another man called out: "Darcy!"

This one was tall and somewhat heavyset, and wore a blue seersucker suit, a white shirt, and a geranium-red tie. And he, too, held a gun, a large nickel-plated automatic. It was aimed in front of him, at the two Arabs. And he spoke to them now: "Back away, or I'll shoot you both."

They froze, watching him. They did not back away, but the one with the gun removed his hand from the girl.

"I will shoot you," the large man said. "I have license and money to do what I want here. I will shoot you both dead and then get on a plane and fly home. I will suffer no consequences. If you don't believe me, stay where you are."

The two men took a tentative half step away from the women.

"Wait," Justine said. She went toward the men and grabbed the briefcase, but the man holding it would not let go.

"No!" he said.

"Let go of it, you fuck," Justine said, and with her other hand she brought up the onyx-handled folding knife that the girl had stolen and pulled from her purse in the American Café in Venice. Justine held the tip at the man's eye. He released the case.

The large man came toward them. Will had gotten to his hands and knees, and was gagging and spitting in the sand.

"Go!" the man yelled. The two Arabs stepped farther away but did not leave.

Justine looked at Little Bitch. The man in the suit was glancing at her, too, without quite taking his eyes off the two Arabs. "Hello, Darcy," he said. She smiled at him. He wore round eyeglasses, and his thinning hair was a fine flaxen blond you don't see in most people by the time they reach adulthood, the hair of a little child. His face was flushed, his cheeks beamed, and the combination of the rosy visage and the hair made him look very young, though Justine guessed that he wasn't. Early thirties, she thought.

The two Arabs had stepped farther away but were not leaving, and the one still had his gun out.

"It's high time," Justine said to the girl. "I'd lose the pack if I were you. Will," she said, "are you all right?"

"Maurice told me," he said.

"I thought he might. Do you hate me?"

"I guess not."

"Darcy—" said Will.

"Go home," the girl told him. "It's time. I'll be in touch." She reached into the bottomless purse and took out a rubber-banded stack of bills, drachmas and liras and sterling, and dropped it beside Will. It looked to be the wad she'd stolen from Maurice in Venice, plus some she'd added.

To the large man in the suit, who was now beside them, Justine said, "Did you see our man back there? He's armed, too. We'll get him."

"No," said the man.

"Can you hold this?" the girl said. She shoved her pack into his chest, which knocked him off balance.

"Run!" said Justine.

Sixteen

WHEN THEY REACHED THE CAR, Karl, who had dozed off, was so startled he didn't know what to do except get out—especially when Justine yelled at him, "Get out!" From the trees, twenty-five or so yards behind them, came the shouts of the men.

"There's a man chasing us!" Justine said. "He's got a gun!"

Karl, in his dopey confusion, lumbered along the pathway toward the trees.

Justine slid behind the wheel and started the engine as the large man emerged from the trees and ran into Karl. Then the two Arabs and Will arrived, and Karl somehow seemed to run into them, too, and there was much shouting and threatening and pointing of handguns. At least that's how Justine imagined it. She couldn't really hear because she was busy putting the car into reverse and spinning it around. She heard no reports, so she assumed they hadn't actually tried to kill one another.

"Wait," the girl said. "Give me the knife." She leaped out, ran to the white Mercedes, and plunged the blade into the left front tire. Justine looked over her shoulder and saw the men still arguing, and then one of them pointing at her. The girl punctured the left rear tire as well and got back in.

In her haste, Justine sped through a group of young travelers, two men and a woman, Americans or Canadians, riding Rent-a-Vespas. One of them, a tall boy with curly hair, had to cut it into the sand to avoid her hitting him, and he pitched forward. She was glad to see in the mirror that he got up and gave her the finger.

As they drove toward the hills, it was Little Bitch's turn to cry. She sat silently, with her head down, and Justine could see her shoulders moving. She reached across as she drove and put her hand on the girl's neck. They were not tears of sorrow or of joy, really, but of relief, Justine imagined. And of the realization just now of how truly close to being gone forever she had come. It was a startling, sickening thing to realize after the fact how narrowly you've escaped an especially black chasm. Justine had felt it before: the heat of a bullet after it passed your ear, the smell of the inside of a Marrakesh police car after being rescued from a converging group of drunken men. And she knew that something had been broken in the girl, or at least shifted. That she would be different in some small way. She couldn't help it. No one could.

After a few minutes, the girl stopped, wiped her face, looked up, and smiled.

As the old Mercedes climbed back into the mountains, headed this time for Iraklion and the quickest possible way they could find off the island, neither of them spoke. Darcy was watching out the side window, wiping at her eyes every now and again. It wasn't until they passed the American military installation they'd seen on the way over that Justine said, "Who was that man?"

"That, I'm very nearly positive, was Matthew Raines, my rescuer, my pursuer."

"The seersucker savior."

"Did you just love the suit or what?"

"I did." Justine drove a little farther and then said, "However did he find you, do you suppose? And just at the right moment."

"I called him last night before Will and I went back to the room. I had this feeling it was time. He was in Iraklion. I said I'd tell him where I was if he agreed just to watch me."

"Or?"

"Or I'd run away again."

"Ah." Justine smiled.

"He'll probably keep coming, you know."

"As will Maurice and those Arabs whose sixty thousand quid we just nicked. Are you happy?"

"That I'm not being sold into white slavery? Duh."

"That's not what I meant."

"You believed that crap back there? 'Oh, Mother. I'm yours. We'll be so happy.'"

Justine looked sharply at her, and now Darcy started to laugh. She said, "You're pretty damned sentimental underneath it all. You know it?"

"I am," said Justine. "Always have been. Can't help it."

"Well, I forgive you." Justine's right hand rested on the gear shift. Darcy placed hers over it and said, "Silly old bitch."

A MONTH OR SO LATER an envelope arrived in the box at my apartment building in Charlottesville, where I'd returned to finish my degree. It was sent by my mother and contained another envelope, this one pale airmail-blue, postmarked Ankara, Turkey. Inside was a snapshot of Darcy and Justine with their arms around each other in front of a huge mosque. Across the bottom in black marker was written *Hagia Sophia, Istanbul.* Along with the photograph were two notes.

One said: "Will—I hope you loved most of it. I think you did, or you will, one day. I love you. You know that. I don't know how. It's confusing. Confused. But it was time for you to go, my sweet boy, and find your life. Godspeed. Justine."

The other said: "Hey, lover. Having a wild time. I'm sure we're under the threat of imminent death from either Maurice or the Arabs, or both. But Matthew's still following me, if you can believe that, so I don't feel scared. Kind of turns me on, actually, thinking about it. xxxooo D."

It was the last I was ever to hear from either of them.

In Matala, I had waited with Matthew Raines for an auto service to come and replace his damaged tires, and so we had a chance to speak. He was a nice guy, if a little miffed that Darcy had duped him and extended his tour of duty, who knew for how long. I gave him an overview of the whole thing from my perspective, and he filled in some details for me. He gave me his card and offered me a ride to Iraklion, but I said no thanks. I needed to just think, not to talk anymore or be around anyone I knew.

I never went back to Maurice's to reclaim my things. I didn't need them anymore. I kept the Matala spoon Darcy had lifted in my pocket for some reason, some kind of good luck charm or something, and that was all I wanted. I still have it.

I hitched a ride back over to Galini and caught a bus north that afternoon.

I like to imagine that what those two women saw and felt when they were leaving was much the same as me. But I don't think it was. I was a looker back.

As the bus groaned up and away from the sea, it passed through a clearing from which I could just make out, to the east, the red cliffs of Matala. I sensed even then that I would probably never see the place again, this ancient coast, this land where stories began. And so I bid it good-bye—but only good-bye in real time, which I had finally begun to recognize as the illusion it was. In other, more important sorts of time I would see this place often again, and I would come to know it in ways I had barely touched upon while actually there. I would know it, and it would come to know me, so that we would meld, finally, into a single being that was not either one of us in life. And then we could begin, each of us, to invent the other.